The Jackals of Babylon

By Matthew Reed

PublishAmerica
Baltimore

First printing

ISBN: 1-60610-642-2
PUBLISHED BY PUBLISHAMERICA, LLLP
www.publishamerica.com
Baltimore

Printed in the United States of America

Acknowledgments

A special word of gratitude is in order for all those whose hard work and encouragement made the writing and publication of these tales possible. First, I want to thank my parents, Debbie and Jerry Reed and my younger Brother, 1st Lieutenant Jonathan Reed, U.S.M.C. for all their kind words and support. To my old high school buddy and Stephen F. Austin State University roommate, Charles Beveridge, thanks a lot bro, for reading and loving the first two stories I ever wrote-don't worry, I won't forget the little people. To all the hard working folks at Publishamerica, thank you for accepting so many manuscripts from a previously unknown author and working with me to get them out into the market.

To my great pals, Britton Stephens, Ray Brock and my brother Marine, Larry Jacksch, I write these tales as much for all of you as I do for total strangers.

To all the Marines I had the privilege of serving with in the 1st Marine Regiment, Semper Fidelis my friends. If America ever ends up "Slapping Leather" with Iran or North Korea, we will likely meet again.

To Mark, thanks for being my best friend since Kindergarten.

To all my Drill Instructors, Senior Drill Instructor Staff Sergeant Armendariz, Drill Instructor Sergeant Neal, Drill Instructor Staff Sergeant Vu and Drill Instructor Sergeant Hussey, thank you for making me into a U.S. Marine so that I could walk across that Parade Deck on January 10, 2004 to Claim The Title.

To the late Gus Hasford, Corporal, U.S.M.C. a great writer, Vietnam Vet and the real life Private Joker, thank you for inspiring me to become a writer.

For everyone else that I've neglected to mention let me just say, thank you.

PROLOGUE

They often live, work and move among us, often going unnoticed to the untrained eye. They often became what they are through rough, hard life experiences or years of intense Military training and combat experience in the Infantry units of the Army or Marine Corps or years spent in Special Operations Units such as Army Rangers, Marine Force Recon, Delta Force and the Navy SEALS. They can be seasoned SWAT Officers turned Security Consultants, or men who become Private Military Contractors overseas after four to eight years of Active Duty in one of the U.S. Military's more prestigious outfits. Either way, each man is part of a fairly unique breed.

He can be a former Serviceman turned professional trigger-puller or high-speed private Military Operator. Or, he can simply be a former Soldier or Grunt who loves Firearms, Marksmanship and shooting and thinks nothing of a fistfight or slinging lead into *anyone* who threatens or attempts to physically harm him. He is not the sort of man who would ever allow a lowly minion of the government to cow or coerce him with any sort of impunity.

Such men are often described as fitting into three animal kingdom-inspired categories: Sheepdogs, Foxes and Wolves. In reality, they are quite different from the so-called "Sheeple" that they move amongst. Some of them may go a step beyond becoming an "Operator" or a "Contractor" and become hired triggermen or even Mercenaries. There are certainly a fair number of such men who take the latter two fields of endeavor. However, as the reader will find, such people, can, in some cases, turn out to be females.

Such a woman could be a former Military Intelligence or Counter-Intelligence specialist turned "Spy-for Hire," who is adept at using her feminine wiles to attain her goals right before she uses a knife to cut her target's throat and bleed him to death. She could be a high-dollar Call Girl, who either "moonlights" as an assassin, or informs her more powerful, wealthy male/government official Clientele of the true power she holds over them after being arrested by the Police, while refusing to suffer the indignities of institutional American legal hypocrisy regarding the world's oldest profession.

As a result of the War on Terror and the Iraq War, there are a much larger number of such men with this sort of experience moving stealthily through American society. There are those "Sheeple" on the Left, the Right and even the Anarchist side that bear a certain amount of fear towards such people that can be classified as Wolves, Sheepdogs or even Foxes. In the former two cases, the fear comes from knowing that Sheepdogs, Wolves and Foxes can and do, have the skills and means to rebel against or resist various idiotic Laws or Edicts, issued by their favorite ruler with "D" or "R" next to his or her name.

While I was going through Boot Camp at San Diego MCRD, one of our Drill Instructors, while waxing philosophical about the current state of affairs, reminded us that no matter how mad most civilians get, or how much they bitch about a horrifying injustice or an indignity, they are, for the most part, all bark and no real bite. It was said that if America is ever invaded or, if the government ever comes to molest us *en masse*, take away our Firearms and what little is left of our Constitutional Rights, it will be the Veterans, i.e. the Wolves, Foxes and former Sheepdogs who band together, organize and take up arms to kick whatever ass needs to be kicked.

Think and meditate on this concept as you read the following tales.

AN AMERICAN ASSASSIN ON SIXTH STREET

A Scott Raines Story

February, 2005. Austin, Texas. Saturday, 12:30 am.

Austin's Sixth Street is a little slice of Revelation's Babylon, the mother of all harlots herself, a veritable new age hodgepodge of alcohol, sex, and drugs combined with high-tech, run down and early post-apocalyptic style architecture inhabited, toured and devoured by everyone from all species of U.T. college students to all types of human breeding experiments gone haywire. When you spend a night in Sixth Street, if you don't end up stewed, screwed or tattooed, you could be skinned and eaten alive by the closet cannibals dressed and disguised as humans who populate many of the strip's various outlets for the expulsion of human suffering. Sixth Street is where college virgins come to cut loose and have fun, but leave as experts in the carnal arts and survival of drug induced gang-bangs.

On Sixth Street, if a driver pulls up and offers you cocaine, you have to remember to stick your head through the patrol car window, blow away the marijuana smoke and say, "No thank you, Officer."

Dressed in my phony beard and ponytail disguise, I glance around before entering the Chained Lust Club. Throughout Sixth Street, throngs of over anxious condom toting youngsters and genetic defects that look like Charlie Manson on LSD, wade through the city's one and only river of darkness as their bodies are washed by the glowing of neon fixtures designed to serve as beacons of light for those who yearn to discover a short term cure for two terminal plagues known as reality and civilization. I shake my head as I step into the Chained Lust Club to briefly meet my contact.

The Chained Lust Club has the overwhelming, nostril-searing scent of a neo-nazi slumber party and barbecue gone mad. It is the end times filth-zone hangout for homosapien perversions who never bathe, an un-caged zoo of vile vagrants, homeless bums, geriatric bikers, chronic masturbators, chrome coated bondage freaks and coyote whores, whose bodily fluids are more hazardous than the content of a viral test tube at the Centers For Disease Control. My contact is somewhere behind the bar. Behind the wet bar it is pitch black except for the flashing lights shining on kinky, chain swaddled, leather clad girls, gyrating inside copper cages to the tune of a death metal song that bears striking similarity to a McCullough chainsaw slicing through a bed of sheet metal. The rear of this Gothic establishment is not only a horror writer's worst nightmare, but a medieval architect's acid-induced vision of the Boiler Room on Hellraiser III. In front of the first cage, dressed as a Hell's Angel, is my contact. As I brush past him he hands me my information packet, which I take to a stall in the club's restroom to read. I start reading. The bathroom has somehow been repeatedly shelled by high explosive artillery, and besides smelling like cocaine coated hog shit, it has that particularly pungent odor of any all male barracks in a Marine Corps Infantry Camp like Horno or San Mateo. In my briefing package are photos and information for both the missing girl I am to find and the man she was last seen with.

I've read all I need to, so I tear up the packet and flush it down a toilet unfit for a Somalian bandit. Across from the Chained Lust Club is the M Club, where Linda Ann Maywald was last seen. It seems she last went into the private room of the club's owner, a sludgebag dope dealer and kiddie porn freak named T-Dog Jenkins. At one time T-Dog was nothing but a common street hustler and pimp. But since he served his Mafia masters and their "wise-guy" subordinates so well, he was rewarded with a position of ownership in one of the local night clubs.

Walking towards the M Club I check the side pockets of my black-leather jacket. On my right side I have a small, miniature cylinder of napalm wired to a timer and a quarter ounce of C-4 plastic explosive. On my left side, in a customized shoulder holster is one of my favorite killing tools and personal negotiation appliances: a black, silencer equipped Colt M1991A1 .45 caliber pistol fitted with a laser sight and three seven round magazines loaded with six jacketed hollowpoints. This pistol's serial number was swabbed away with hydrochloric acid two nights ago and I had thoroughly wiped down the shell casings and their bullets while wearing two layers of surgical gloves. There is one bullet now in the chamber. Its magazines are loaded with only six rounds so that they'll have an extra push from their springs and thus lessen the chance of any inconvenient stoppages. The holes in the bullets are filled with triple X gunpowder and formulated mercury sealed with wax-a highly explosive combination. Under some other circumstances when doing a "hit" job I would have preferred a Ruger .22 caliber automatic with subsonic ammunition. But tonight's scenario as well as the opposition that I'd be terminating would call for something just a little bit bigger. And just in case I need it, I have a well-forged Austin Police Department I.D. and badge hooked to my belt with the badge facing out and tucked into my blue jeans. If my briefing packet was correct, T-Dog Jenkin's "office" was soundproofed; however, I won't know this for sure until I actually step inside of it. This mission will be risky, but I need the money, and I have great faith in my compact, yet amazingly accurate Colt firearm. Colt pistols are some of the most reliable weapons ever made, and besides, thugs like T-Dog are never as tough when up against armed professionals as they are around kidnapped girls or their mugging victims.

God may have created Men, but Americans like Sam Colt made them equal.

The M Club's admission is five dollars per person. I step into a quasi-futuristic world that is as alien to me as intelligence is to a California Valley Girl. The M Club's sterile, metallic-silver, plasmatic inner organs glow and radiate bright blue light which illuminates multiple echelons of sweaty figures and heart shaped asses slithering, cringing, bumping and grinding as if they are stuck in a swamp dodging reinforced battalions of striking pit vipers. Pushing my way through a perimeter of human freakazoids to get to the bar, my ears finally take notice of their torture by the club's colossal stereo system, which is blasting out computerized circuit noise that sounds like a parade of Cape Buffalo stampeding through a nitroglycerin plant. After bursting into and out of a pack of George Romero zombie impersonators, I reach the club's wet bar. Only, it doesn't look like any bar I've ever seen before.

The bar is a Space Shuttle repair shop and a future android's fluid replenishment station covered with all the accessories of a female cyborg's makeup kit. The kitty-cat of a bartender turns towards me and is wearing on her face, mouth, nipples, ears and various pubic areas what appears to be the better half of an intergalactic hardware store. The young bartender is a demented science fiction writer's wet dream. Her dress is what you would wear to go dancing at a sleazy, high-tech, nightclub if afterwards you were planning on auditioning for the part of a prostitute on a Star Trek movie. The Sci-Fi bartender says; "What'll ya have Man."

I say, "a Bud."

"A what," she screams over the M Club's brain bashing sensory bombardments.

I say, "A Budweiser, you know, a beer"

The bartender says, "Sorry pal, we ain't got any of that shit, but here's what we do have." She fires off an endless list of exotic species of stress numbing liquids that I've never heard of before and whose names sound as if they belong in the inventory of a Bio-Chemical Warfare Lab rather than on a nightclub's menu.

Frustrated, I say, "Just give me water". She fills a glass for me.

"No charge for water." she says.

I whip out my badge and quickly flash the forged I.D. with my picture on it in front of her face. Then I pull out the picture of Linda Ann Maywald. I say, "Seen her before?"

She says, "Yeah, she was in here about two nights ago. Two nasty lookin' dudes took her up to see the owner, but no one saw her leave. It looked to me like they each had a pretty tight grip on her arms and she looked scared."

I say, "Where's the owner at?"

The highly informed girl points way up and to my right. I look that way and see through a dark hallway, a neon-laced, gold trim door on the elevated, and very *secluded* third floor of the club.

I say, "Thanks," and head up a set of perforated steel stairs to give Mr. T-Dog a warm, lead filled interrogation. As I do so, I slip on a pair of black leather gloves.

The M Club's collective volume drastically increases as the noise bursting out of its speakers reaches a scrotum splitting crescendo. Rapid-fire strobe lights and pulsating laser beams emanating from the ceiling, rape the club's promenade and dance floor making them look like the business end of an

AC-130 Spectre Gunship's air strike on a Taliban bunker. Looking behind, I see that the first and second floors are a polluted sea of jumbled, indistinguishable shapes. Excellent. As I move closer to T-Dog's private room I see that there are three guards around it and although I can't gaze far enough into the club's chorus of flashing chaos to glimpse the one in front of the office door, I can easily see the two that are the closest. The two bouncers nearest to me are any mirror's worst nightmare.

The first bouncer is a neck-less, steroid pumped Jamaican brachiosaurus with gold-banded dreadlocks thicker than those worn by the Predator that Arnold Schwarzenegger destroyed at theaters in 1987. The Jamaican clasps his hands in front while flashing me a shit-eating grin and I see that covering his teeth and fingers is more precious metal and jewelry than Cleopatra wore on her first date. This island beast looks like he could rip open a Grizzly Bear's skull and eat Gonja weed after sucking its brains out. The second bouncer, a gargantuan Chicano with an eye-watering body odor affliction, is the perfect cross-breed of a Latino hatchet murderer and Jabba The Hutt. The blubber consumed Chicano is the type of guy who wipes his ass with chunks of broken concrete and uses rusty machetes for toothpicks. They eye me with suspicion. Time to launch the offensive.

I kick over the table the Chicano is seated at, launching crack-needles and razors into the air and onto Mr. Lard Tub. Jumping forward, I begin to raise up my left leg to kick him in the knee. When the Chicano grabs at my left leg and misses, I bury the steel toe of my right cowboy boot into his crab-infested genitalia, crushing a nut. As he collapses, I punch him hard in his throat before open-handedly smashing the bridge of his nose upward into his skull. He falls back, smashing tables and burying himself in debris as I start to draw my pistol. The Jamaican is huge, but not too swift. I turn just in time to see him barreling my way and I instinctively react as he starts to wrap his industrial size arms around me in a crushing bear hug. Turning into his attack with my left shoulder, I shove my thumb through his right eye only a split second before using my right hand to ram my silencer barrel up under his sternum and pull the trigger three times, blasting his Cro-Magnon heart into hamburger chunks. He tenses in conjunction with the bullets exploding inside his chest cavity before his body goes limp. The Jamaican grunts like a pro-football linebacker getting crushed by a steamroller as blood gushes from his throat onto my shoulder. I push the soulless carcass to the floor and turn to go see that Mr. Jabba the Chicano remains down for the count. Sure enough, he's flat on his back grabbing his flabby neck and swollen balls. I swagger over to his refuse-caked body and put one round through his forehead before turning to finish my job.

Directly in front of T-Dog's door is the last pathetic excuse for a guard. He is a squirrely, 95-pound, white as an Archangel's toothpaste, fucked up punk rocker with a green maggot infested lump of queer Aztec headdressing for hair. His looks and facial features make it apparent that his mother was a deformed peacock impregnated by Beavis and Butthead. He is jamming out next to a boombox the size of a C-5 Galaxy military transport on steroids and is wearing a black T-shirt that says "Masturbate Now, Avoid The Plague."

I kick over the punk rocker's stereo and as he tries to throw a punch at me, I grab and twist his right wrist back before barreling into him and ramming his pasty body up against a wall. He tries to resist, so I quickly slam my left knee into his groin. He gasps and tries to slump forward. I grab the little bastard's slimy hair, spin him around and place my Colt .45 against his head before twisting the silencer's barrel into his right cranial temple and drawing blood-screwing in the right combination for green hair's compliance.

I say, "On your knees asshole!"

Groaning and gasping after the frontal assault on his nuts, Green Hair complies and I force him onto the floor face first and spread eagle. Gus Hasford was right, many people in this world are like old TV sets: they have to be beaten upside the head before they get the picture. I leap up slightly and with all my weight, bury both knees into Green Hair's back, knocking the wind out of him. While kneeling on his kidneys, I quickly eject the first magazine and slip it into the left rear pocket of my blue jeans before inserting another one and chucking a round into the chamber. I grab his hair again with my left hand and even with my gloves on, it feels like I'm trying to get a grip on a bush-like pile of Martian pubic hair coated in extra-terrestrial semen. I straddle Green Hair and slam the silencer's barrel back where it was before yanking up on his hair and as he reluctantly rises up, I place my mouth right behind his ear.

I say, "What's your name shithead?"

The slime encrusted, white twig of a crack-baby says, "Punky."

I say, "Listen up Punky! If you don't do exactly what I say, I'm going to rip out your eyes, skull-fuck you and blow your goddamn head off!" And answer every order with Yes sir! Understood?"

Punky says, "Yes sir."

I say, "Punky we're going to see your boss. Now open that door, follow my orders and I'll let you live"

Punky says, "Yes sir," and opens the door while I use him as a shield. We enter and before his boss can look up from his desk, I lightly kick the door shut. No outside sound can be heard. The room is definitely soundproofed. I trip Punky and slam his limp noodle body right onto T-Dog's crack-covered desk. CRASH! The desk falls forward and Punky is smacked by desk and floor in turn. T-Dog looks up, a look of shock on his bloodshot eyes. I have the drop on T-Dog with my Colt .45.

I say, "Punky stay there!"

Punky says, "Yes sir."

T-Dog Jenkins is a jewelry-plated, gold ring-banded, purple-suited flamingo of a street hustler. The gold chains and necklaces hanging over his neck and chest are thick enough to hold up a 60-ton main battle tank dangling from a Blackhawk helicopter. Stuck inside the band of his violet fedora are assortments of peacock feathers. To T-Dog I say, "Put your fucking hands up by your head and step to the right of that desk or kiss your life goodbye motherfucker!" My laser sight's red dot is centered on T-Dog's chest. He does just as he's told. It's so wonderful what a man can accomplish with a kind word and a gun. I pull out the photo of the missing girl.

I say, "Her name's Linda Ann Maywald, and she was last seen being taken to this office with you. Now where the fuck is she?"

T-Dog says, "Goddammit, don't you be comin' in here wit dat kinda attitude kickin my cracka' ass bitch around and trashin my dope you white mothafuckah, I could have yo' neck broke by one o' ma' homies on da' street wheneva' I say!"

I say, "Put a sock in it fuckrag, I've got the gun and I do my own neck breaking to cut down on my expenses. Now where the hell is the girl?"

T-Dog says, "Punky, get up and stab this honky bastard fo' I fire yo' pale ass."

I say, "Punky"

Punky says, "Yes sir"

I say, "Punky stay down and keep your goddamn mouth shut!"

Punky says, almost crying, "Yes sir." I notice a shut closet behind T-Dog.

I say, "T-Dog, what did you do with the girl. Lie to me and you'll be shark bait!"

T-Dog says, "Fuck you, you white ass redneck, I ain't never seen that ugly-ass bitch befo'. Why don't you just suck the black off ma' big-ass cock!"

I center the laser sight's red dot on the bottom of T-Dog's right thumb.

I pull the trigger. *Crack* Boom! The silenced Colt .45 recoils and T-Dog's entire right thumb shatters, explodes and disintegrates as blood splatters and spews all over his arm and soaks his purple pimp suit. The gold ring that was on that thumb has flown off and landed somewhere else. Damn, I love making my own ammo.

After freezing in wide-eyed surprise and shock with that "oh my god what the fuck just happened" look on his face, T-Dog collapses to his knees and cries out in inhuman agony: "Aaaaaahh, oh, mothafucka, oh shit!!! You chuck bastard, you honkey mothafuckah, I fuckin kill you, oh fuckin God, fuckin shit, my fuckin hand, I swear I fuckin kill yo' sorry ass, you pig, I kill you crackah, I kill you!!" I smirk and chuckle. T-Dog's fancy, feathered violet fedora just flopped to the floor and his anger is writing checks his body won't ever cash. Poor T-Dog is sweating, howling, yelling and shaking like a little blue Hungarian midget crapping out a wad of spike-tipped bowling balls.

I say, "Now, what about the girl?"

Grunting, panting and sobbing, while violently gripping the jagged maw of bloody flesh where his right thumb used to be, T-Dog quakes, gasps, takes a deep breath and says, "Ok, ok, ok, she come in here a couple of nights ago, and I done fucked her skinny ass! But that's all, I swear man, I fuckin swear that's it!"

I say, "What's in that closet?"

T-Dog says, "Nothin man, oh God, leave me alone, ain't nothin in there!"

I say, "Bullshit, now stand up cockpuke!" T-Dog leans back and stands up a little.

Crack Boom! *Crack* Boom!

I shoot T-Dog twice in his left foot. Shoe leather, blood, viscera, toenails and bone fragments are blown out all over T-Dog's carpet and phony

Leopard-skin rug. To the casual observer, T-Dog's left foot would appear to have been run through and then yanked out of a turbo-charged tree shredder.

T-Dog writhes in excruciating pain and screams like a prom queen being hacked up in an 80's slasher movie.

I say, "Punky."

Punky, says: "Yes sir."

I say, "Punky, get up and open that closet door right fuckin' now."

Punky says, "Yes sir", and opens the closet door. A clear plastic body bag containing Linda Ann Maywald's bloody, mutilated corpse comes tumbling out along with a stack of unmarked videos.

I say, "Punky stay right there."

Punky says, "Yes sir."

For a moment T-Dog's pupils widen to cosmic proportions as he looks at the transparent, blood saturated cocoon of a body bag.

T-Dog is squealing, crying and huffing and puffing while groping his macabre wounds. "Please, mothafuckah, oh please" he says. "I just did what I be told man. Hey man, take the bitch's body, she just another crackhead ho, I swear, I ain't goanna tell nobody bout' you, just take the ho's body and leave, don't kill me whitey, I be square wit you. Me and some o'my homies done fucked her a lot and we cut her up and we done filmed it. Now I be tellin' the truth goddammit, come on, cut a brother some slack man!!!" I move my laser dot onto T-Dog's forehead. He cringes like a scolded puppy.

Punky says, "I have to shit."

I say, "Punky, shut the fuck up and tie a goddamn knot in it!"

Punky says, "Yes sir."

I say, "Well, T-Dog, I've never been any good at showing mercy and besides, you're of no use to me now." T-Dog starts to quiver, scream and moan like a kidnapped damsel in distress being given a vertical hysterectomy by a chainsaw-wielding maniac from Texas. I shoot T-Dog in the head.

POP, SPLUTCHH!

Instant nanosecond phantasmagoria. The top half of T-Dog's head now bears an uncanny resemblance to a watermelon that just gave birth to an exploding grenade. The wall behind T-Dog appears to have survived a grape throwing contest. I turn the Colt on Punky.

I say, "Punky, from now on you can shit out of your head." I shoot Punky in between the eyes, killing him deader than a clump of expensive fish guts on a cruise-line cracker, finishing the job that his drugs were doing. Punky has just shit his brains out. I glance at the corpse of the eighteen year-old fox turned "snuff" victim. Life really is a bitch.

When I leave and get picked up by my "associates," we'll give our customers the bad news, but first things first. I pull out my slender, mini-napalm cylinder mated with C-4 and set the timer for eight and a half minutes. I push the ARM button on the timer, exit the room and calmly shut and lock the door behind me as I walk away from the Club's isolated third level, and beat feet down the stairs to the M Club's rear exit on the first floor.

Wading through the dancing, interwoven strands of genetically altered human fashion displays on my way to the exit, is like visiting an extra-terrestrial zoo made up of kidnapped humanoids from all corners of the galaxy, whose bodies and clothes have been contorted to fit into some alien scientist's bizarre mating experiment. Before opening the exit door my attention is caught by the M Club's most attractive attractions. Inside giant bird cages, pinned up on raised platforms, the grooving seductresses are slender, black spandex clad, fully blossomed hourglasses of flesh wrapped in eye scorching white luminescent tendrils of transparent plastic which highlight their snakelike body movements. Underneath artificial pulsars, the glossy Black Widows continue prick-teasing every male creature in sight as if preparing for some ritualistic after-hours orgy.

I grin as I step into the totally darkened, deserted alley beside the Club. I'm all alone. I open up the nearest manhole before disassembling my Colt .45, and dumping it, along with all of the parts, magazines, ammunition, holster, phony police I.D. and knife, down the sewer. Even if, by some astronomical chance, the police were to somehow get hold of the pistol's barrel, they wouldn't be able to match it to the bullets since the hollowpoints had deformed and exploded shortly after penetration. I trot to where the alley meets the street and look at my watch. Reaching down to grab the square plastic holder clipped to the right side of my belt, I remove my walkie-talkie, a Radio Shack model 21-1861, 14 channel, 2-way radio and switch it on before uttering the right set of words to get the ball rolling. I can hear the vehicle coming. My comrades in arms drive by and pull me into a dark blue Ford van with tinted windows that says "Loomis Plumbing Inc." on both sides. The van's interior remains shrouded in darkness since the circuits that power its interior lights have been cut out and removed. They're all wearing plumbing uniforms while carrying fake IDs and sporting professionally fashioned wigs and mustaches. They toss me a set of Loomis Plumbing coveralls to immediately change into, just in case we get stopped and searched by any local law enforcement personnel. If any of the city's badge wearing minions do, by some chance, catch onto us, we'll know about in advance due to a handy piece of modern scanner technology.

Mounted on the console in between the two front seats is an eight hundred Megahertz, PRO-433 Triple Trunking, police and emergency services band scanner. That we had bought at Radio Shack.

Two nights ago we had slipped into an old junkyard on the north side of the city and found a set of matching license plates just sitting there on the ground. Since these were now on the van, we wouldn't have to worry about any of the intoxicated witnesses nearby taking down our plate numbers and giving them to the police afterwards. The radio transmissions that we hear about ten minutes later state that an explosion has occurred at the M Club and that a fire is rapidly consuming part of it.

We drive until we escape the maw of taboo satisfaction and reach the outskirts of Austin. Just outside the city, we drive into an old garage owned by Michael Bechtol, one of our old comrades in arms from our time in South Africa. Once inside we park the van and strip off our disguises. We'll let Michael wipe out all traces of evidence and disassemble the vehicle in his machine shop. All of us then take separate cars out of Austin with myself heading east on 290. I'll cut up and dispose of the gloves in a roadside trash can at one of the rest areas along 290. Once the explosion at the M Club was registered with the emergency dispatchers, they would send the fire department there in full force. After the firefighters got through evacuating the Club and hosing down the fire they would have trampled on and soaked any valuable forensic evidence. We've accomplished our mission, so I relax and think about Sixth Street. Tonight and for many nights afterward, the surrounding population would hurl itself into the inferno of pleasure excreting constructions that was Sixth Street.

Genesis states that God created the world and all things in it within seven days. He should learn to take more pride in his work and not be in such a rush.

THE END

THE EXECUTIVES

Friday, July 28th 2006. 6:17pm. 22878 Holly Creek Trail, Tomball Texas.

Michael Chatsworth walked calmly to the end of the winding concrete driveway that snaked its way from his two-story home to the main road of the upscale Holly Creek subdivision. He didn't normally go out to get his mail this late in the afternoon but the passing of time had made him ever more complacent. The worst of the death threats had long ago been dismissed by the Police as the work of either another "crackpot" or the tantrums of a disgruntled employee who had lost all of his or her 401K when Gavron Energy Inc had literally collapsed overnight. That collapse, and his involvement in it, was the reason why he had received so many death threats and had originally been slated to stand trial for his complicity in the corporate collapse of the Houston-based energy giant. That collapse had cost thousands of hardworking, middle class people both their jobs and retirement savings. Once Chatsworth realized that as Chairman of the Board for Gavron Energy, he would likely be one of the people to "fry" over the whole fiasco, he had scrambled to cop a plea with the prosecuting attorneys.

Without hesitation, Michael Chatsworth starting "dropping dimes" on

Lewis Clay, the corporation's C.E.O., Arthur Andrews, the Vice President, Mark Svenson, the Chief Financial Officer as well as Lisa and Thomas Jastrow, the husband and wife accountants who Gavron Energy hired from a reputedly shady Houston accounting firm called Amos and Andersen. Even now, years later, the whole Gavron collapse fiasco still garnered national headlines as millions of people still exhibited intense interest in what the outcome of the trial would be next week. Chatsworth had overheard such discussions at CiCi's Café near the Academy Sporting Goods Store in the center of Tomball. In between sips of coffee, one man had commented that it was "such a damn shame" that so many small and large shareholders had lost out and practically been robbed blind along with the company's employees. The older man sitting across from him responded by saying: "Yeah, ya' know, if there was ever a justification for taking out a bunch of contract hits on some people, this is it!" If only Chatsworth and his accomplices who he had "dimed" out had any idea just who else had thought the same exact thing.

What none of them had known before they "cooked the books" and paved the way for the company's financial ruin, was that at the time, a few of the shareholders had been C.E.O.'s of some small time private security firms. Each one of these firms had quickly morphed into massive, global Mercenary enterprises that ended up raking in astronomical profits with the advent of the wars in Afghanistan and Iraq. They hired ex-police and retired military specialists and Special Forces operators to do contract work for both the Coalition Provisional Authority as well as large corporations like Halliburton and Brown and Root, who were currently engaged in trying to rebuild Iraq. Some of these private mercenary outfits like Dark Skies Security, had branch offices in Central and South America where some of their more secretive customers were in fact members of large drug cartels.

It just so happened that one of the kingpins of the Cali Cartel had owned shares in Gavron Energy. That, combined with the fact that some of the C.E.O.s of the security firms genuinely ached for revenge, would ensure that neither Michael Chatsworth nor the others directly responsible for the company's collapse would live to see the end of July.

On the other side of Holly Creek Trail, clad head to toe in camouflage and laying flat on his stomach behind clumps and swaths of thick bushes and brush, Chris Mathews, a,k,a, "The Mailman" sweated in anticipation of what was about to happen. He loved doing shit like this. He had gotten into it after he caught his girlfriend Maggie, cheating on him with some preppy college boy at the University of Houston. Mathews had originally planned to surprise her by visiting her apartment with a box of chocolates. When he arrived, Mathews found her giving a deep throat blowjob to the slimy prick who had an effeminate presence about him. After the bastard fled the apartment half naked, all Maggie could say was that Ricardo, the college student, was "a good listener." Mathews ended up using his skills as a Demolitionist for a local construction firm to teach Maggie and Ricardo a lesson. He mailed each of them a cardboard package containing a moderate amount of TNT inside a can of gasoline. An exploding fuse similar to those found in military issue hand grenades had been inserted into the blocks of TNT with the metal rings they were tied to taped up under the packages flaps. When Maggie and Ricardo had opened the "care packages" after seeing each other's address on them, their hands were blasted apart while their faces and upper bodies were partially crushed and incinerated. "That bitch and her prissy faggot boyfriend didn't stay fucking pretty for long," Mathews had thought afterwards when he laughed himself to sleep at night. Hell, he reckoned that a few days after Maggie opened her "package," she must've ended up looking like Freddy Krueger in drag.

But that was neither here nor there.

Chatsworth was about to get an even bigger dose of what Chris "The Mailman" Mathews could dish out. When Chatsworth yanked open the mailbox's front flap and leaned his head down to look inside after wondering whether or not it was the real, Postal Service mail carrier who had flipped up the red, metal arm on the side, he unknowingly sparked the igniter on a piezoelectric fuse wired to roughly six pounds of Semtex plastic explosive. "WHAPBOOOM!" The sound of the explosion reverberated throughout the entire subdivision's pine scented air, sending perched birds speeding out of trees and making neighbors inside their homes pause with utter shock.

The blast nearly disintegrated the mailbox as it blew shards of metal and wood into Chatsworth's chest and stomach while simultaneously turning his head, neck and upper chest cavity into a bursting balloon of partially incinerated, bone, flesh, muscle tissue and charred brain matter. Half-incinerated bits of Chatsworth's cerebral cortex, followed by high velocity skull fragments, actually ended up battering the tree trunks in front of Mathews and he struggled to contain his laughter as Chatsworth's battered corpse twisted and twitched in the wind as if trying to find what the hell happened to its head and neck, before crashing onto the asphalt road a split second later.

Mathews low-crawled backwards out of the tangled thorns and brush he had been hiding in and ran deeper into the woods where he had stashed his motorcycle. He quickly put on his black helmet, flipped down the visor and sped out onto a dirt road at the rearmost section of the heavily forested neighborhood and came back around on Holly Creek Trail and calmly cruised away from the scene of the crime on the way back to his West Houston apartment. His killing of Michael Chatsworth would help set decisions into motion that would end up making it easier for the rest of the Executives involved in Gavron Energy's destruction to meet their maker.

1238 Beamer Road, South Houston. 10:45 pm. Two nights later.

Susan Riley, a.k.a. "Charisma" skillfully whipped her red BMW around the narrow lane off Beamer Road and parked parallel to a small but elegant one story, brick house. She knew that the house's insides were both upscale and opulent as it belonged to one of her wealthier clients, a forty eight year old, former Gavron Energy financial manager named Brian Chalmers. Susan had conducted her first "session" with him about eight weeks ago. After the whole Gavron scandal began, and Brian Chalmers's name was splattered all over the city newspapers with all of the other higher ranking corporate masters already implicated, his reputedly promiscuous wife left him for another woman. Soon afterwards, Brian had been charged and given a distant, future court date with the other executives. He recently decided that he needed certain forms of stress "relief" and began looking for an Independent Contractor on various local Escort agency websites in Houston. That was when he found Susan Riley, whose official Escort name was "Charisma." She was a true expert in the arts of carnal pleasure and since Brian Chalmers was, if anything, a creature of habit used to secure routines, he began "seeing" her on a regular basis for five hundred dollar "sessions" every Sunday night. This had gone on for the last eight weeks like clockwork at 10:45 pm. After she arrived, he would hop in her car and they would drive out to an abandoned construction site on Unity Drive off Westheimer Road for some teeny-bopper style fucking and sucking. These bouts of intercourse made Chalmers feel young again.

Following such a routine made the job of the professional killer parked catty corner down the street so much easier. Seated inside his black Dodge Plymouth, retired Army Ranger Nick Steiger watched his target's house and skillfully eyed his unsuspecting prey through dark, tinted windows.

After Chalmers entered Susan Riley's car, the two of them sped off down Beamer and turned onto Fuqua towards I-45. The black Dodge Plymouth maintained a healthy distance while traveling north on I-45 and the 610 Loop. As they cruised past South Post Oak and neared Beechnut Street, Nick Steiger smirked and tightened his black gloved hands on the steering wheel. Not getting caught killing someone was a major concern now that he was plying his trade *inside* the United States. Still, in the end, he knew it was nowhere near as hard or as rough as the missions he participated in when he "cut his teeth" in Afghanistan killing the Holy Hell out of packs of worthless Taliban shit bags. Upon reaching his End of Active Service Date in February 2004, he went to work for Dark Skies Security. Thus far, the private sector side of killing was proving to be quite lucrative. Getting paid twenty grand just to kill these two lovebirds made him ecstatic. Fucking Army never would've paid him that much for any mission, no matter how hazardous.

Fuck 'em, he was banking now.

He worked hard to maintain his distance after following his targets left on Westheimer while going through the Galleria district. When Susan Riley turned left on Unity Drive, Nick Steiger kept going straight until he reached South Gessner, at which point he turned left and then headed east on Richmond Avenue. Upon reaching Unity Drive, he hung a left and slowly cruised up near the back of the abandoned construction site that the two fuck rats were using for their private sex getaway. He turned off his headlights and slowly turned into an old dirt parking lot surrounded on three sides by thick, overgrown bushes and shrubs. He parked behind an old set of porta-johns to help hide his car from any occasional driver that might happen by. While starting a reconnaissance of the area a few nights before, Steiger had also noticed that the space behind the "shitters" gave him a wide, fairly unobstructed view of the entire construction site. Now, he could see his targets parked in front of an old, gutted, two story steel structure, making out and steaming up the windows.

He stripped off his leather jacket and slid into the top half of a thin, green jumpsuit he was already wearing and zipped it up tight before pulling a balaclava hood over his face and fastening an AN/PVS-7B night optic device, a.k.a. a "Seven Bravo" on his head. He clicked it on and the nightscape turned into a far more visible world bathed in bright green. Next, he grabbed his M-4 Carbine, slapped in a twenty-five round magazine with wiped down shell casings and racked the charging handle back, chambering a soft nosed 5.56mm bullet. Steiger then reached down and turned on his PEQ-2A laser sight and watched its beam project straight and true through his night vision goggles. The PEQ-2A laser sight shone in a spectrum invisible to the naked eye and could only be seen with night optic devices like those he wore. Reaching down near the floorboard, he yanked out the circuit box where the internal lighting wires connected. After tying a drop bag with two extra magazines around his waist and screwing the foot long silencer in place over the barrel, he decided he was ready.

While Brian Chalmers continued to enjoy his executive fuck session, Nick Steiger left his Dodge and scurried while hunched over, to where the line of bushes met the gutted building. He flicked off the M-4's safety catch and glanced around in a 360 arc, carefully scanning for both unusual movement and any odd heat signatures.

So far, so good.

Keeping an eye on the red BMW through a gaping hole in the building's rusted frame, he skirted around its east side and pressed his left shoulder up against one of the bare supports. The BMW was starting to rock back and forth. Sounds of pleasured moaning and grunting were escaping into the chilly, windswept night air. He took a deep breath and slowly let it out, counting backwards from ten, to slow his heart rate and calm his mild adrenaline surge.

Inside the BMW, Susan Riley slipped a condom onto Brian Chalmer's dick and carefully slid him deep inside her womanhood. She wrapped her shapely legs around the back of the chair and began to viciously grind on top of him. Her client didn't seem to care that she was faking the build up to an even more fake orgasm. Death began to close in on them.

With the Carbine's stock pressed hard into his right shoulder and his left hand keeping a death grip on the "broom handle" support underneath the barrel, Steiger snuck in behind the car and brought himself up next to the driver's side. He kneeled down and leveled the green laser's beam right on the middle of where Susan Riley's head was moving up and down. He thumbed the selector switch to "BURST" and fired. Dull popping and cracking sounds mixed with breaking glass pierced the night as three .223 caliber rounds were stitched up and down Susan Riley's jaw and head, blasting out tiny, concentrated divots of flesh, bone, brain matter and blood all over the car's windshield. Her body slumped and started to twitch. He fired another three round burst, sending the soft nosed bullets boring through her mouth, throat and forehead. Her head jerked back again and for a split second, Steiger thought he could hear her wheezing and trying to scream, as a string of skull viscera oozed down her left shoulder.

Brian Chalmers started to scream and panic, desperately trying to push the spasmodic, dead woman's body off of him after her bowels emptied themselves on his legs.

With cool, methodical efficiency, the killer stood up, turned around and angled the PEQ-2A's rod-like laser beam onto the center of Chalmer's chest. His target stopped moving and gazed up at the unbelievable sight that assaulted his eyes.

"Oh my God, p-p-please, don't k-kill me," he stuttered.

Nick Steiger fired a burst into his pleading target's chest right before putting another tight grouping right through his fore head. He reached inside and examined the wounds. He checked each one for a pulse. Nothing.

He crouched low and ran back behind the uncompleted, rusted monstrosity and jumped back into his car, stripping off his killing implements and driving back onto Unity Drive. Now, all he had to do was dispose of everything he had worn, boots, hood and all. He had fulfilled his end of the contract. Now he could pick up his money and wait for another contract. Steiger chuckled to himself when he thought about what undoubtedly lay in store for Chalmer's fellow cronies. That ought to be fun to read about.

Friday, 11:48 pm. 2222 West Loop South. The International Hotel.

With the preliminary hearings in the trial now over with, the remaining Gavron executives and their two chief accountants would be returning to their homes for the night in style, driven to their respective destinations and dropped off by two professional ex-Limousine Drivers, who were even now, waiting patiently for their customers behind the steering wheels of two thinly armored Lincoln Navigator SUVs. Neither Chuck Taylor or Jim Miller had expected to land a job driving these preppy Gavron swine around, but the shooting of Brian Chalmers compounded with the mailbox bomb that blew Michael Chatsworth's head into oblivion scarcely two weeks ago, had made it happen. Those assassinations had convinced local Law Enforcement authorities that the lives of all the Gavron defendants were being threatened. Thus, during the week, Lewis Clay, Arthur Andrews, and Mark Svenson, along with Lisa and Thomas Jastrow were kept sequestered in the Intercontinental Hotel. They were only allowed to go home on weekends where they all had private bodyguards in their Bellaire and River Oaks mansions for protection. So far, nothing bad had happened and all seemed well, but Jim Miller and Larry Taylor knew better. Tonight it would be very different indeed.

Taylor and Miller each had their own financial problems that were literally eating them alive. For Taylor it was the gargantuan medical bills that had been racked up for his daughter's cancer treatment at the M.D. Anderson Clinic in the Houston Medical Center. In Jim Miller's case, it was the messy, ongoing divorce with his bitch of a wife. Such money troubles had made each man a prime target for bribery and recruitment. One week ago a lone man had approached the two of them with the promise of easy money to pay off their bills. All they had to do was wait until the night of Friday, September first, and simply alter their normal driving route so that they could bring both vehicles onto Westheimer just north of West Alabama Road and drive them down Yorktown Street to be placed directly in between a small, square city block filled with oak trees and an upscale apartment complex.

The trim, physically fit blond man who gave them these instructions handed each of them a small, white envelope with one thousand dollars inside. He said it was just a "good faith deposit." Afterwards, the muscular, blond man who had looked to be in his early forties, made it crystal clear to both men that if they spoke a word of this to anyone, both they and their immediate family members would be brutally murdered. Taylor and Miller saw no reason to test the accuracy of the man's warnings, so they kept their mouths shut and decided to exactly do what they were instructed to do. How could they afford not to? When the more inquisitive Miller thought to ask if something bad would happen to Taylor and himself since it seemed to him like someone was setting up a "hit" of some sort, the blond man just smiled and said not to worry. He assured them that whatever happened would be made to look like an accident and the two drivers would have their asses covered no matter what, etc, etc. Taylor thought the mysterious man was doing his best to be sincere. If only they'd known the truth.

Taylor saw movement out of the corner of his eye and turned in time to see Lewis Clay, Mark Svenson and Arthur Andrews coming towards his Lincoln Navigator. He stepped out and opened the rear passenger doors for them and then hopped back inside to start up the engine. Miller did the same for Lisa and Thomas Jastrow. As Taylor drove out of the Hotel's parking lot and turned onto South Post Oak Road with Miller following suit, he picked up the tiny Trac-Phone the blond man had provided and dialed the cell number he had been given. A humorless voice answered, "hello."

"Charlie said he'd take Gina out to the Foxy Hottie tonight," responded Taylor.

"Fuckin awesome bro, we'll be there," came the voice from the other end before it clicked off. Chuck Taylor tossed the phone onto the empty passenger seat and paid no attention to the rapid-fire arguments and legal chatter of the three corporate thieves seated behind him. So far, none of them seemed to notice that they were following a totally different route than the one they usually took. Neither Taylor nor Miller noticed the red Honda Civic that came to life behind them as they both turned right onto Westheimer and cruised past the Galleria Shopping Mall.

Inside the Honda Civic, retired Marine Sergeant Roger Schulke took great care to maintain a reasonable distance between his vehicle and the SUV Miller was driving. He calmly reached over to the center console and lightly gripped the stock of the fully loaded, silence suppressed, M-4 Carbine before grabbing the cylindrical frame of the M-203 grenade launcher underneath its barrel. Feeling it so close by gave him great piece of mind, as it often did during his service in Iraq with 1st Battalion Fourth Marines, where it never left his side. As soon as the two Lincoln Navigators turned left onto Yorktown Street, Schulke grabbed his Motorola Walkie-Talkie before pressing the "send" button and verbalizing the warning order. "Stand by, stand by," he said.

Further down, parked at the corner of Hidalgo and Yorktown in a white Ford F-150 with phony City of Houston decals on the doors, Tyler Lerma pressed the send button on his Motorola radio three times to let Schulke know that the message had been received and to put out the final preparation order to the two fire teams that were already in position on Yorktown just a little north of Fayette Street. The police band/emergency channel scanner hooked to his dashboard was clear as far as any urgent Law Enforcement activity was concerned. No one appeared to have noticed Michael Ruzinsky and Thomas Hawkins driving by earlier and shooting out the bulbs with a silencer equipped Ruger .22 pistol. Thus far, their recent appearance in the middle of the night to start fixing the non-functioning streetlights on this section of Yorktown Street seemed to have attracted little or no suspicion since they were all dressed in official blue City of Houston coveralls with matching blue hard hats, their weapons having been disassembled and placed inside large toolkits purchased at a hardware store in Arcola. By now, they would have fully assembled their chosen killing tools and busted out the necessary night vision optics. Tyler Lerma just hoped it could all be done fast enough.

Positioned slightly south of where Fayette Street intersected Yorktown, former Marine Anti-Tank Assaultmen[1] Seth Seppala and Oscar Ramirez knelt down after the two "squelching" sounds came out through their earpiece communicators and made ready to fire the Russian made RPG-29 "Vampire" rockets at their intended targets. The round that was now loaded in the launcher tubes were Thermobaric variants of the more widely made 105mm HEAT (High Explosive Anti-Tank) munitions. Essentially, when the main warhead detonated after punching through a wall or careening off a protrusion in an enclosed space like a cave, it would first throw out a mist comprised of both the primary explosive elements and combustible aluminum. That thick mist would be ignited barely a millisecond later, producing both a far more powerful explosion and unbelievably more lethal overpressure than conventional high explosives would if delivered in a warhead of the same size as that of the Thermobaric[2] rocket. Seppala looked through the heavy 1PN51-2 night vision sight attached to the rocket launcher's tube and waited patiently, his bicep muscles and hands tensing and flexing in controlled anticipation. On the other side of Yorktown, kneeling diagonally from Seppala and Ramirez's position, retired Marine Sergeants Mike Brasher and Nick Drazst took long, deep breaths, exhaling slowly to control their increasing adrenaline flow. All four men had complete confidence in the primary weapons platform they had chosen. During the recent Israel-Lebanon war, Syrian backed Hezbollah fighters had used the HEAT round for the RPG-29 to a somewhat significant effect against Israeli made Merkava IV Main Battle Tanks. The tandem charge at the tip of the warhead effectively neutralized much of the ERA (Explosive Reactive Armor)[3] that the Israeli Defense Forces placed on its tanks. Properly placed shots in vital areas of the tank often took care of the rest.

Inside the lead SUV, Chuck Taylor assured Lewis Clay that the only reason they changed routes was for security; i.e, making it harder for anyone stalking or following them to guess where they would go next. This assuaged Clay's worries and allowed Taylor to concentrate on carefully crossing West Alabama Street. He slowed down to barely 5 MPH and once he saw Fayette Street appear, he turned off his headlights and almost literally drove the black Navigator at a snail's pace, just as the blond man had instructed him to do. Taylor and Miller each hoped that this wouldn't be too painful.

After the lead Navigator flicked off its headlights and continued to inch forward, Seppala and Ramirez leapt out from where they'd been waiting and kneeled down directly in front of the first SUV. With Ramirez clutching his MP-5 submachine gun and holding his AN/PVS-7 night vision goggles up to his eyes to quickly san for any signs of trouble, Seppala sighted in on the vehicle's windshield through the mild, green haze of the night sight. Once he had a clear sight picture, Seppala pulled the trigger and sent the 105mm rocket roaring out of its launch tube assembly, the horrendous back-blast smashing the windows of nearby parked cars.

Chuck Taylor's mind barely registered the silence-crashing roar of the rocket's launch before the protruding, tandem explosive charge of the warhead made the initial contact with the center of his Navigator's bulletproof windshield and detonated. A high velocity, flesh-ripping shower of thick glass fragments literally shredded the right side of Chuck Taylor's body. The main charge of the Thermobaric warhead flew by the bucket seats in the front and tumbled in the air before blowing itself open and releasing the misty explosives mixture. When the primary charge of the warhead detonated, it sucked all available oxygen out of the air, raising the temperature in the SUV far above that of any human body's heat threshold and almost totally disintegrated the entire upper body portions of all three executives when the blast radiated outward. Lewis Clay, Arthur Andrews and Mark Svenson were literally smashed, compacted and virtually incinerated all at the same time, while parts of their lower bodies and torsos were simultaneously crushed into the rear seats and floorboards. Taylor's right arm was blasted apart with one whole side of his face and head ruptured like a club-battered watermelon. For anyone watching, the bright flash of light and eyeball-searing heat amidst a skull-battering *BOOM* would've seemed almost instantaneous.

Jim Miller watched his friend's SUV get blasted open and partially incinerated barely a split second before Mike Brasher emerged from the west side of Yorktown Street and fired off his "Vampire" rocket into the center of the right side of Miller's Navigator. As before, the initial tandem charge easily punched through the bulletproof window. Thomas Jastrow's head and neck were turned into a bloody Sushi cocktail before the Thermobaric charge burst open and detonated. Thomas and Lisa Jastrow's bodies were almost instantaneously burned and nearly liquefied by the intense heat and blast overpressure whose inhuman lethality was only magnified by the enclosed space of the SUV. The full on explosion that blew parts of the vehicle's frame outward obliterated what had already been incinerated and crushed. Jim Miller suffered a fate similar to Taylor's as his skull and brain were smashed and blown into the dashboard while his upper body was violently twisted around and practically buried in the driver's side door.

Behind the carnage, Roger Schulke, who had hung back at a reasonably safe distance, brought the red Honda Civic to a screeching stop north of Fayette Street right before stepping out of the vehicle and flipping up the quadrant sights of his M-203 grenade launcher. With the weapon's stock pressed tight into his right shoulder, he sighted in on the ruptured, smoking rear of the vehicle and pulled the trigger behind the cylindrical breech and sent a 40mm High Explosive Dual Purpose round right into Miller's Navigator, blowing up and shredding the remains of the corpses inside. Off to his right, Nick Draszt did the same thing to Taylor's SUV and the explosive result was almost the same except that a fuel line was ruptured somewhere and the vehicle burst into flames. With his final part in the mission done, Schulke jumped back into the Honda Civic and sped off back towards West Alabama Street, the sickly sweet smell of burnt flesh and cordite lingering in the air behind him. Had any pedestrians actually walked by and been able to completely see the two SUVs, they would've glimpsed what looked like two gigantic, square marijuana "bongs" that had been smoked, torched and smashed by some sort of monster the size of a doped up Godzilla.

The other four men knew the rockets and grenades had done their job, so they wasted no time in pulling the pins in the delayed fuse Thermite grenades they had hooked to the large rocket launchers, thereby insuring that the primary tools used in the "hit" would be melted beyond recognition.

With that done, Brasher and Seppala hopped on the black motorcycles which had been hidden in the bed of the pickup truck that was sporting the phony City of Houston emblems. Once the engines of the motorcycles roared to life, Draszt and Ramirez jumped on the rear of their respective bikes and latched onto their teammates waists, holding on tight as they sped south all the way down to where Yorktown Street intersected McCulloch Circle. A modified City of Houston semi-truck was waiting with two sets of steel ramps deployed for them to use. They drove the motorbikes right into the semi's short tractor-trailer and hit the kill switches on the engines as the rear door was slammed shut with a bang. All four of them breathed a sigh of relief as Julio Ortiz, the driver they hired for tonight, put the truck in gear and pulled away from the side of the street. Tyler Lerma smiled as he flicked on the orange caution lights mounted on the roof of the Ford truck and threw it into gear, leaving the carnage for others to sort through.

Off in the distance, police sirens, the lullaby of every major metropolis, wailed like banshees and pierced the sweltering fabric of the hot summer air.

When the "hit" was completed, the proper message had been sent and a fair amount of justice dished out for crimes committed. As an end result, no more hearings would go forth in a now unnecessary trial and some crooked executives would perhaps think twice before "cooking the books." Meanwhile, a young girl in Houston would be condemned to an earlier death from the ravages of one of the plagues of the 20th and 21st Centuries. A philosopher once said that everything contains its opposite.

There it is.

THE END

DEAD MAN'S PARTY

A Scott Raines Story

April 2005. Stephen F. Austin State University. Friday, 2:45 pm.

Another destination, another mission and another target. Nacogdoches, Texas, is a vast pine expanse gutted and sliced into incoherent green quadrants by parallel strips of concrete coated asphalt set beside cracked sidewalks and forests fused with structures of artificial masonry that sustain the lifeblood of the city. The East Texas sun beat down upon Stephen F. Austin State University scorching all that lay beneath its boiling glare. Son of a bitch, it was so damn hot that I wondered if the faces the campus blondes had painted on would melt and flow to the pavement, creating the worlds first and only river of Clairol. Sorority girls in particular were an interesting phenomenon, and by this time had officially been inducted into their respective sororities, receiving not only their own Greek logo T-shirts, but cosmically-inflated egos to boot. No doubt about it, sorority girls had rapidly accelerated the arts of extreme bitchiness and snobbery to record heights previously held by genetically ignorant, and uppity Los Angeles Valley Girls and Beverly Hills BMW matrons stricken with terminal P.M.S.

The collective self-esteem of the campus sorority girls is matched only by the exponential amounts of lust exuded by the tightly packed herds of frat boys who ogle the girls on their way to class while they dream of hunting in the virgin bush. As I sit upon the bench outside the McKibben Education Building, I think about what I have seen while spying on my current target, a Russian terrorist, named Yuri Bratchenko, alias Dan Marshall, a member of the Chi Phi Phelta Thi Fraternity. Yuri, a master hacker who had been trained to speak flawless English by the KGB before he supposedly went "rogue" had been masquerading as a computer science grad student and since he came here had managed to steal three prototype nuclear weapons schematics from the files of the QuadCore Corporation. Yuri was believed to be "lifting" these files in order to sell them to an infamous Arab terrorist organization called Islamic Jihad.

Understandably, QuadCore didn't want their Pentagon patrons to know how piss-poor the company's security really was, since, if they did, they might lose any prospective military contracts, which of course, means losing lots of money. Therefore, they had hired me to kill Yuri, the problem himself, and recover the stolen documents, which I believe to be inside his room at the Chi Phi Phelta Thi Fraternity house. For the past three weeks we had been trailing and watching Yuri Bratchenko to learn not only *his* schedule, and personal habits, but those of his closest friends as well. Tonight, at the Chi Phi Phelta Thi Fraternity house there will be a party and the guests will be their sister sorority, Alpha "Cunnilingus" Omega. I will follow him from his last class to Hall 16 where he usually goes to meet his buddy, Chip Van Wiggam, before going to a party.

At 2:50 pm, hundreds of students burst from the surrounding buildings and fill up the forum outside Steen Library. Amongst them, leaving the computer science auditorium, is Yuri. Almost a minute after he passes by, I put down my copy of the school newspaper and casually shoulder my backpack in order to get up to follow him. Keeping an eye on Yuri is an excruciating challenge due to the fact that after class lets out, the campus is overrun by an ocean of post-summertime bathing beauties, naked for everything but their clothes, who sport platinum manes of hair set above anti-gravity breasts whose shapely clarity absolutely, positively demands that any testosterone based organism within a hundred feet focus its full attention upon valentine-candy asses belonging to ebony princesses and ivory hardbodies. I tail Yuri at a distance into the bowels of Hall 16's fourth floor to make sure that he and Chip really are going to their fraternity party tonight, and besides, I've got to take a piss. On the way, I am nearly run over by two vehicles of opposite extremes: a Chevy pickup truck with tires big enough to fit on Godzilla's go-cart, and a Buick whose occupant is jamming out to a RAP (Retarded Attempt at Poetry) number that sounds like a gong-thudding re-mix of a Los Angeles gang bang and a wedding ceremony in the Congo.

Near room 457, I hear Yuri and Chip talking about tonight's party and playfully discussing the complicated intricacies involved in doggy styling drunk girls without getting a disease or knocking them up. I've heard all I need to, so I nonchalantly ditty-bop over to Hall 16's restroom. As always, the floors of Hall 16 are ankle high aggregates of useless refuse, half-eaten food, and crumpled garbage resulting from a trash accumulation held by America's future leaders for whom picking up after themselves is clearly a health hazard. I chuckle as I walk into the bathroom. Anyone who thinks that America's future is not in jeopardy, should visit a college campus sometime and take a real good look at the slovenly shit-heads who inhabit its dorms. Taking a leak in a Hall 16 urinal involves visiting a professional smut graffiti convention. All over the stalls and walls, our nation's new-age pogue lifers have carved, scrawled and written words and passages that would make

South Central Los Angeles's oldest, saltiest whore blush with all the fevered embarrassment of a sixteen year old country girl receiving an uninvited grope for the first time from a horny, small-town jock. After washing my hands I decide that it's time for this mission to enter the final stage of execution.

11:30 pm. The Nacogdoches nightlife has officially croaked. I awake from my rat sucked bed in the roach-brothel, Highway Motel on North Street before showering, putting on my black jumpsuit and strapping on all of my night camouflage clothing and "mission-oriented" gear. Beneath my left shoulder strap is a silenced Beretta 9mm, loaded with hydra-shock hollow points. Slung over my back and right shoulder is my primary weapon, a silencer equipped, Colt M4 Carbine with the carrying handle removed for the placement of night optics. This weapon is a shorter derivative of the AR-15 assault rifle, complete with five 30-round magazines (not loaded to full capacity to help prevent magazine stoppage) stored in nylon pouches on my left side. Each magazine is loaded with Remington .223 caliber Polycarbonate ballistic tip bullets. The silencer on its barrel is an eight inch, matte black titanium Viper suppresser with 1/2 by 28 inch threads designed to fit onto the rifle's muzzle flash hider for fast, easy attaching and detaching. As usual, the serial numbers on all these tools have been scorched off with hydrochloric acid and the shell casings have been carefully wiped down. Besides packing a Ka-Bar knife, I have a tightly rigged backpack with several plastic squirt tubes of gasoline, and three chunks of homemade incendiary explosives rigged to three propane cylinders. Also in my rucksack, is a remote detonator for each bomb, a 4-pound canister of sodium thiopental[4] aerosol, two white phosphorus grenades and four thermite grenades. Dress for comfort but pack all the firepower you can handle, a valuable skill for modern life. I gaze into the bathroom mirror to think and reflect.

We become professional Hit-Men because it's easier than remaining visible, because we are too sharp, tough, ugly and mean for the feminized, pussy-whipped, normal, schoolmarm world to handle. We are angels of death who strike and murder before vanishing into the folds of infinity sewn into father time's invisible cloak. When ignorant executives, crime-syndicates and pussy ass politicians can't achieve jack shit through diplomacy, they call us to get results. We are the *real* troubleshooters. We fix troubles by shooting them. Logic may work on some people, but fear and pain inflicted by the hands of trained killers through highly effective weaponry works on everyone. Violence is the language that even the dumbest, craziest jackasses will be able to comprehend. I look at my weapons. The magical power involved in possessing a gun hasn't changed since the Spanish Conquistador Hernando Cortes blasted and barbecued Montezuma and the Aztecs. Give me all your precious gold or I'll shoot your fucking idols and perforate your precious temples. The Good Lord giveth and the assault rifle taketh away.

The power of a gun is the only true equalizer. Any lone, pretty young female packing heavy firepower in a bar full of sexually erect males is not a piece of meat, but a respectable woman. A shot through the air will grab anyone's attention as quick as a suitcase full of money. Peace comes through superior firepower. The elites have big bucks, and the middle classes have big guns. The East Coast Ivy League yuppies and West Coast Rolls Royce Rambos have high rise buildings, while middle class hunters possess high caliber rifles. Firearms and ammunition are so wonderful in their ignorance and lack of caring. All that a bullet knows is that today's desirable Cassanova is tomorrow's corpse of the month at the county morgue. Money talks, shit walks and weapons communicate. I chuckle. In the mirror on the bathroom door I resemble a perfect mixture of humanoid space alien and cat burglar combined. I am the Grim Reaper, the soul harvester, hidden beneath a pseudo-covering of human flesh. I shoot an assault rifle, therefore I am.

I step outside and get picked up by my fellow "associate", Ray Brock, a former U.S. Army Counterintelligence Specialist, ex-Houston Cop and pussy hound extraordinaire. We turn left on North Street in a dilapidated Ford pickup truck, a common and rather inconspicuous sight in Nacogdoches.

Ray says, "Hey man, you made any more alternate escape plans.?"

I say, "Yeah, why?"

Ray says, "I heard that theses QuadCore cocksuckers were the ones who hired Jack Trask to do that botched job in Dallas and then gave him a hollowpoint lobotomy."

I say, "Don't worry, Ray, I'll watch my back. Just make sure the rest of the guys detonate those explosives all around Angelina County on time."

Ray says, "Roger that, good buddy."

We turn left on East College Street and get treated to the finest examples of the college population. Flying by us at warp speed in Ford Mustangs and Dodge Vipers are more perfume permeated, makeup armored sorority chicks packing miracle-bra enhanced bosoms and wearing various shorts and mini-skirts, each in turn short and tight enough to permit any long distance observer with binoculars to conduct a thorough gynecological examination of their lower abdomen. Inside the campus "quack shack" infirmary, squads of sweet, innocent, recently deflowered, loose kitty daddy's girls are picking up their daily supplies of birth control pills. The things that would happen if only mothers didn't keep secrets from their daughter's fathers.

On the sidewalk beside Steen Hall is the show of the night. A platoon of aristocratically reared, senior sorority matriarchs are leading a smaller detachment of freshman pledges on a meat parade, passing all of the other mere mortals with their noses turned up high enough to catch the jet turbines of over-flying 747's in a sort of "I'm better than you pass-in-review," as if to say "we are superior to everyone else and we've got wine in our piss, so stay out of our way all you non-fraternity noodle-dicks!" The senior sorority sisters are 8th-degree black belts in the arts of whining, bitching, leaching, adultery, and male libido manipulation. Directly behind them walk their younger freshman sisters. They are peach skinned, pixie-faced, eighteen-year-old tightbody sex-kittens who could tongue-lash a popsicle with all the finesse of a thousand dollar a night call-girl working overtime in the bedroom of a Las Vegas Casino. Sorority girls would marry a mutilated dildo if it had Greek letters on the outside and gold on the inside. We pass the second stop sign going towards University Drive.

As we scoot by William R. Johnson Coliseum, I look to my right and see a tender young teen angel vigorously flirting with a pack of fraternity brothers. Her looks and demeanor identify her as another naïve country flower. The ignorant girl thinks that she'll be able to cock-tease lust mad, post-pubescent, acne-scarred, horny-happy, Rohypnol carrying sexual psychopaths with the same skill she exhibited in the beds of pickup trucks while seducing adolescent corn-shuckers and teenage cattle ropers. She's nothing but a bloody mackerel in a sea of hungry sharks. To our left, across from the Coliseum, two University Police Department heroines known as pistol packing Annie and Smith & Wesson Susie are courageously risking their lives to write parking tickets for the twelve thousand students who have trouble fitting into six thousand parking spaces. U.P.D. also functions as the campus revenue service. It would be impossible to spell the word stupid, without the letters U, P and D.

We turn left on University Drive and hit Austin Street before turning right.

We drive about three miles east and then Ray stops and lets me out into the woods. I trot through the striated forest of Nacogdoches pine trees until I am directly across and somewhat catty-corner from the Chi Phi Phelta Thi house. On the inside, the Nacogdoches forest is an emerald formation of reptilian-scaled vines, intermingling branches and bark coated wooden columns guarded by luscious green fauna sprouted above an ocean of fallen brown mini-spears.

I watch and wait, looking through my detached Mk. 6600 series night vision scope. Inside the house, yet another fraternity/sorority social gathering (breeding ritual and mating fest) is about to enter its final stage. The bowels of the house take on a life of their own as excess guests leave, and Lusty Lucky Lukes prepare to mount their lively Lolitas at a breakneck pace, and I have a front row seat courtesy of AMT Night Vision products.

The house is a choppy inferno of orgiastic proportions. Boys grunt while girls moan as the exuberance of their primal instinct increases in speed and volume. The sounds resonating out of the house are the echoes of a regiment of hyperactive crack babies sucking on pacifiers in unison. Eventually, they are all finished and being tuckered out, begin falling asleep. Heavy doses of Jack Daniels and Mary Jane Rottencrotch puts these people out like a light. Two more minutes of observation time have passed. Inside his room on the second story, Yuri is sleeping through the residual afterglow created by pumping his girlfriend.

1:45 am.

It's time to move. With my rifle pulled tight against my shoulder, my entire body and soul wired as tight as a pair of thong lingerie bottoms on virgin pussy, I crouch low and slip out of the woods until I reach the rear of the fraternity house. There is an open, inflow air vent directly in front of me. I sling back my rifle and un-strap my canister of Sodium Thiopental, stick its rubber outlet tube into the duct, and turn the mini-handle, pumping the chemical vapor mixture into the house's ventilation system, the circulating anesthetic gas being breathed in by the occupants. Much like Ether, Nitrous Oxide is a highly potent "inhalational anesthetic"[5] and is often used by physicians and dental surgeons to rapidly put their patients to sleep before being surgery begins. It is colorless and emits a sweet odor sometimes leading to mild hallucinations and euphoric behavior, which is why it's been nicknamed "laughing gas." I got the idea for this little stunt from Vince Flynn's awesome novel: *Term Limits*.

After eight minutes, I re-pack the canister, move up to the back door. I turn the doorknob, it rotates completely and the door slides open. The hinges on the door are brand new, so they don't squeak. So much for the can of WD-40 I'd bought.

I step in and shut the door.

The Colt Carbine is pulled tight into my shoulder, my eyes alert and bearing down on the iron sights, as I smoothly sweep my rifle from side to side and silently bound up the stairway. I reach Yuri's room and it is open. Yuri and his petite playmate are sound asleep. After stealthily slipping into his room I shut the door and lock it. The blonde on Yuri's bed is stark naked, legs akimbo. You know, come to think of it, when spread open, a girl's twat closely resembles a fuzzy shrapnel wound cavity.

I raise up the Colt rifle and fire a two rounds first into the blonde's head and then Yuri's, soaking the bed and its pillows with skull fragments awash in brain matter. Sweet dreams motherfuckers.

Cracking open Yuri's safe and swiping his handful of computer disks is easy enough and all the stolen documents are right there. I stuff them into my backpack before placing a remote detonated bomb near Yuri's desk and then soaking his room with the gasoline from my squirt canister.

Suddenly, that old gut feeling of impending doom racks my brain like a bullet through a brick. Something is wrong, but I'm not sure what. I had told my micro-managing QuadCore patrons that I would exit the frat house out of the back door that I came through. Why they had originally wanted such detail, I wasn't quite sure, so I had thought up an alternate escape plan. I would go out the sliding glass door at the front.

Eyes and ears alert, the arterial hellfire of adrenaline coursing through my veins, I leave Yuri's room and slunk down the stairway squirting and soaking everything in sight with gasoline, including the hot water heater, under which I stick my second bomb. I pocket my squirt tube, hoist up my rifle and sneak towards the front door, while carefully avoiding the unconscious Greek princes and their sleeping beauties. On the way, I come across a large shelf and take notice of the fraternity's diverse video collection of sleaze flicks and hard-core pornography. Included are such illustrious titles as *Sexy Horny Women Minus Clothes, Little Suzy Does 'em All, Peggy Sue Gets Anal, Lesbian Love Triangle, and Cannibalistic Vampire Vixens Tortured by Carpathian Sadists.* I sling my rifle and slip into the house's kitchen on my right and inspect the gas stove. I turn all six of the burners on "high" and soak the surrounding areas before placing my last bomb next to the stove and moving to escape.

I open the sliding glass door and begin to make a dash for the road where my next "associate" will pick me up in about thirty seconds, but turning to look back at the house, I see something move on the roof. Someone is on top of it. I brace myself up against the wall of the house, sneaking around to the other side where I saw visible movements. I sidestep away from the brick wall with my rifle raised toward the roof to see what's up there. A man gripping a Heckler and Koch MP-5 submachine gun is aiming down towards the back door that I entered through. Son of a Bitch! I see only his right side.

He jumps up and turns in my direction. Somehow he must've heard me sneaking up on him. He tries to turn and shoot me, but he hasn't passed his final exams on that course, so I pop off three shots sending three Remington ballistic tip rounds through his chest. His body crumples like a toothpick under a D-9 bulldozer and rolls off the roof before I can put a third one into his skull. I race to his body and strip off his ski-mask and see the face of Chance Boudreaux, one of QuadCore's security chiefs and an amateur idiot. The rumors about what happened to Jack Trask must've been true. Jack Trask had been hired by one of QuadCore's "big-wig" executives to kill the man who was fucking his pretty, young wife. Some of us had heard that when Trask had completed his job, the executive who had hired him changed his mind about how to deliver the second half of the payment for the job. Rumor had it that the executive in question told Trask to meet him at some out-of-the-way location so he could deliver the money. It was said that when Trask showed up, three Pinkerton security guards in plainclothes armed with MAC-10 Uzis poured out of the executive's limo and gave him a chest full of Hydra-Shock complaints. The banshee squeal of braking tires on asphalt screams through the air.

I run to the black Dodge pickup on the South side of Austin Street. I hop in and Ray speeds off as I rip off my ski-mask. A few seconds later, I pull out my remote detonator and punch the "detonate" button. KABOOM! Behind us, someone has tried to insert a Petro-Chemical explosion into the Chi Phi Phelta Thi fraternity house. Future Yuppie barbecue extravaganza! Ray looks over at me and says, "What the fuck were you doing over by the side of the house!"

I say, "It's a fucking setup. That motherfucker I shot was Chance Boudreaux, a QuadCore security chief. He was waiting for me above the back door, it's gonna be a fucking trap, just like they did to Jack Trask!"

"Well fuck me," says Ray. "What do you wanna do?"

I say, Are all the explosives around Nacogdoches and Lufkin setup?"

"Yeah, they're all ready to go."

I say, "How far ahead of schedule are we."

Ray says, "Exactly five minutes."

I say, "Good, then drop me off in the woods across from our scheduled rendezvous point."

"Ok, any bright ideas?"

I say, "Pick me up just as we planned, same place and time in about twelve minutes, and tell Danny to have that helicopter ready to go at G&S Lumber Yard a couple minutes early. We're gonna have to move really fuckin' fast."

Ray says, "Roger that."

I say, "I have a hunch that Chance Boudreax was going to meet our Lexicore friends where they were supposed to meet us. If they show up, I'll show'em what a hard bitch payback really is. Be ready when I signal you guys to set off the bombs that are planted around town."

Ray says, "Fucking A, you got it."

I say, "There it is."

Ray slams on the brakes as I jump out into the woods on the north side of Starr Avenue across from the Mobil gas station next to Grogan's Cleaners, our rallying point with QuadCore's Chief Executive back-stabbers. If they show up, they'll be expecting to see the late Chance Boudreaux. But instead, they'll meet their maker. I slip into the brush and move towards the ditch until I can see the Mobil station. I un-sheath my encrypted cell phone, punch in the proper numbers and then hit the send button, letting out a communications signal that would launch Armageddon for an entire section of East Texas. Everywhere throughout Lufkin and Nacogdoches, except for any place near University Drive and Highway 59, are fire-bombs planted in closed restaurants, closed factories and abandoned buildings and warehouses. The signal from my phone is the "green light" for my "associates" to set off all those incendiary explosives with their remotes. I take my Mk 6600 AMT night vision scope and slide it onto my rifle.

The stagnant night air of Nacogdoches is ripped open, pierced and ravaged by over thirty-six explosions. Far off in the distance, balls and tongues of smoke and flame dissect the dark sky forming glowing gashes in the air as dozens of man-made structures are swallowed and incinerated by mother nature's burning killer. Prometheus the Greek fire-bringer has come to town. Right now, my "comrades" are using local pay phones to call in phony bomb threats. In the process of doing so, my friends would claim to be part of any number of Arab terrorist groups. With the police, firemen and E.M.S. units scattered around the countryside, away from University Drive, I am left to my own devices. I came up with this simple idea for a diversion while I was reading Richard Marcinko's awesome novel, "The Rogue Warrior." After about ten minutes a couple of fire engines and ambulances go by. Then, about eight minutes later, a glossy black Lincoln limousine the size of an aircraft carrier pulls into the Mobil station. The side of the limousine that contains the gas tank flap faces towards me. The middle doors open up and out walk three young, beauty-parlor-manicured, steroid-bloated guerillas in three-piece suits, with arms the size of branches on a mythical Greek god's Christmas tree-Linkerton security guards. The Pinkerton trio are tanned beach bum Nazis acting both tough and relaxed.

I pull my weapon to my right shoulder, wrapping the rifle's nylon sling around my left forearm and elbow, lining up the scope's bright red crosshairs on the gas tank cover. The two Linkertons are opening the limo's rear doors for their corporate bosses. I take a deep breath, gradually tightening my squeeze on the trigger, my right eye peering through the scope as I center its reticle on the gas tank covering. I slowly let out my breath, squeezing harder on the trigger. The sounds of six flying projectiles exit my barrel with short, audible "*cracks*" as six Remington ballistic tip bullets burrow into the vehicle's fuel supply. The Linkertons barely have enough time to pull out their MAC-10s and drop down into a Weaver firing stance, before WHAPBOOOOOMM! The oversized Lincoln bursts outward into hundreds of burned pieces as a gigantic wall of flame followed by a shrapnel-filled shockwave incinerates everything within about 15 feet, creating an instantaneous roadside bonfire. The Linkertons are shredded, roasted and blasted into the air, one of them landing directly on Starr Avenue. Since the fuel lines are cut off after closing time, the gas station is only partially damaged.

I sling my rifle and sprint forward, grabbing the faceless, black husk of a security guard and dragging him back to the inferno. I look at my watch, only one minute now. I must destroy as much evidence as possible. I strip off all my guns and gear, including my black jumpsuit until I am wearing nothing but a white T-shirt, socks and blue jeans. I set aside the squirt tubes of gas, along with both white phosphorus grenades, all four thermite grenades and my last propane bomb. I stand back and toss everything else into the evaporating limo, including the two Linkertons. I pull the pins on the four thermite grenades and hurl them into the car's charred, flame infested skeleton. I set the timer on the propane bomb for one minute and thirty-seconds before pulling the pins on the two white phosphorus devices and dropping them on top of the cast-iron caps covering the gas station's fuel reserve. Soon, very soon, the grenades will melt through the fuel caps and make contact with the underground fuel supply.

I walk onto the road and stand face to face with a white Chevrolet van sporting Stephen F. Austin State University maintenance shop markings on it. The side door opens and out steps another of my "associates," Nigel Stokes. He hands me a four-gallon tank of "fu-gas" (gasoline mixed with liquid soap creating a type of homemade napalm) onto which I duct tape my propane bomb. I run to the ditch and toss it into the section of piney woods where I had previously been. This will make a hot little forest fire. We run into the van, slam the door shut and take off, going exactly the speed limit heading west on Starr Avenue towards North Street and Highway 59. I look back at the Mobil station, and WHUSHBOOOM! It is disintegrated and devoured by a sea of subterranean flames. I change into a pair of university maintenance coveralls and pin on my fake, campus ID badge. Fire trucks, police cars and ambulances are about to become the dominant land feature in the Nacogdoches-Lufkin area. We laugh and share a little bit of mercenary banter.

At the G&S lumber yard next to the Agri-Supercenter tractor dealership on Highway 59 north, we strap explosives timed to go off in four hours onto our van's gas tank and jump into the helicopter with "KSNL-13 News" markings on it. Danny Soliz, our helicopter pilot, executes a vertical take-off and elevates our souls into the dark, charcoal tinged sky. Once inside the chopper, I proceed to unscrew the silencer before running a rat-tail file in and out of the rifle's barrel until I've scratched up its inside pretty good. Just in case the barrel was ever found this would prevent any ballistics matching with the bullets. After we land at an abandoned, private airstrip 50 miles southeast of here, we'll bag up all of the carbine's components and dispose of them in a variety of locations up and down Highway 59 and I-45.

We've succeeded in our mission and issued out a little revenge. The evidence has been burned into oblivion along with the frat house whose occupants are now certified crispy-critters. We are crude, but slick and effective. To engage in the black arts you must always go the extra mile. In politically correct terminology I am emotionally challenged and suffer from acute deficiencies in sympathy and mercy. Some would just say that I'm evil. Well, different people excel at different things. I excel at creative assassinations. Love never had my phone number. Sympathy lost track of my address along time ago.

Below us, the pine-shrouded terrain is an ochre ashtray sprinkled with the glowing cinders of orange dragon breath, strangled by flashing tentacles of blue and red halogen. Danny turns around and flashes me a "thumbs up." I return the gesture, my mind pondering what my heart and hands have done. I grin and smirk.

How well will I sleep tomorrow night? When the Grim Reaper has nightmares, does he dream that he is giving life to unborn babies?

THE END

BLOODHAWKS AT DAWN

July, 2007. 8:53 pm. 3775 Wilshire Boulevard. Los Angeles, California.

Standing behind the Metro Rapid bus stop canopy next to the intersections of Wilshire Boulevard and Western Avenue, the Contractor took one last look at the imposing structures lining the streets. Considering the careful and meticulous planning that had already been completed for this operation, it probably wasn't absolutely necessary for him to be here. Still, he wanted to take it all in one last time, just in case something changed or was about to change. It all looked as it had in weeks past: the Liltern Theater, the Lupus restaurant next to the Theatric Makeup School and the Kids Land on the ground level of the Pierce National Life Building to his right. There were clearly no new surprises as far as last minute city street construction was concerned.

In the morning, everything would be good to go.

He nonchalantly turned to walk around under the makeshift pavilion that had been erected over the Wilshire/Western Purple Line subway entrance. As he descended deep underground on the escalator, he carefully eyed every human being going the opposite way, looking for any telltale signs of undue suspicion.

No one even acknowledged his presence and he received no eye contacts or fleeting glances. This was most likely due to the fact that he was a rather ordinary looking man with close cropped black hair and a tall, relatively average build that fit nicely under the collared shirt and blue jeans he was wearing. Still, those simple clothes covered a toned, physically fit body which bore its share of scars from eight years of Active Duty in the United States Marine Corps, the last four of which were spent in the elite First Force Reconnaissance Company headquartered at Camp Pendleton, California.

After leaving the Marine Corps, he had gone on to work as a Human Intelligence (HUMINT) Specialist in the Defense Intelligence Agency. Two years into the Iraq War, he had started seeking related work in the booming Private Military Contracting industry. A notable, yet highly discreet risk management/private military firm known as Optimum Solutions had hired him to work in one of its highly secretive divisions which specialized in performing outsourced, "black bag" contract work for the whole range of three letter intelligence agencies. Not unlike his time in Marine Force Recon, his years working overseas for the D.I.A. had taught him the value of blending in and not being seen. As he stepped off the first escalator and descended down the next, it was obvious that his skills were paying off yet again.

He sat down in one of the hard, marble chairs and spent a few moments doing his best to look totally relaxed. As he gazed up at the ceiling of the cavernous platform above him, he found himself musing about the first goal to be achieved in tomorrow's mission. That goal was to brutally assassinate a Qatari oil billionaire named Abdallah Khan. Abdallah Khan publicly embraced Western vices such as sports cars, movies, alcohol and even supple, elegant European call girls whose pleasure-giving talents he seemed to crave. Yet in private, he was in fact a Wahabbism-supporting Muslim radical who regularly sent millions of dollars a year to terrorist groups like Yassir Arafat's Fatah faction and Islamic Jihad. However, it was ultimately his recent funding of branches of the Iraq insurgency that finally landed him on the shit list of just the right sort of powerful Intelligence official. It was Abdallah Khan's money which had allowed other supporters of the Iraqi insurgency to purchase enough materials to construct the ultra-deadly Explosively Formed Projectile Devices that could penetrate tank armor and had already maimed and killed a number of America servicemen.

The Contractor wasn't exactly sure *who* had ordered and agreed to finance tomorrow's hit on Khan and he really didn't care. He wasn't paid to care, only to plan, organize and execute the mission and in that he had already done quite well. In fact, he had managed to set up a fast assassination operation with only a handful of independent contractors plus a pair of truck drivers and two prototype weapons, both of which he felt quite certain were surreptitiously obtained by the same powerful intelligence official who had contracted him to do this job. The first part of the mission would be completed shortly after 7:15 am tomorrow morning when Abdallah Khan's lightly armored limousine followed its usual route into the city's upscale Westwood district.

The Contractor's thoughtful reverie was broken by the purple line subway cruising up to the edge of the platform. He sat down on the plastic chair at the far end of the subway car he'd entered and carefully watched those coming in behind him before a computerized voice announced: "Doors closing."

He stayed on the purple line for quite some time as it shuttled back and forth between Wilshire/Western and Union Station, constantly watching to see if he either saw the same person staying on with him throughout all the back and forth stops, or the same people getting on or off. The Purple Line subway route had proven to be just perfect for this type of counter-surveillance maneuver.

Satisfied that no one had followed him on to or into, the subway system, he finally exited at Union Station and strolled up layers of stairs and escalators before turning right at the end of the concourse. He calmly strode up another escalator to the ground level where he walked to a small booth, paid four dollars to board the LAX Flyaway bus and traveled to LAX where he exited at Terminal Two. He waited another thirty minutes under the green Flyaway bus marker across from the USO and boarded the next bus there and back again, still watching to see if he was being followed.

He pulled a similar maneuver four separate times with the twenty four hour blue bus that shuttled between the airport and the Four Points Sheraton where he was staying.

So far, it seemed that no one had been following him. But that was only because the Professional that was after him already knew where *he* needed to be to accomplish *his* mission. The Contractor was totally unaware of this as he drifted off to sleep inside the Sheraton.

7:11 am. The intersection of Wilshire Boulevard and Western Avenue.

Bill Crawford turned right onto Western Avenue and brought the white delivery van to a slow halt on the shoulder next to the subway exit. His palms were sweaty and his hands trembled as he killed the ignition. It wouldn't be long now.

He looked out the window to his left and saw his partner, Jim Kowalski, turning his van into the street side parking spot next to the Pierson National Life Building across the street from the Coffee Leaf Café. Under normal circumstances, Kowalski parking a delivery van that size at the foot of a corporate office building might seem unusually suspicious. However, official City of Los Angeles Public Works Department decals were emblazoned on the sides of both his and Bill Crawford's vehicles. Since there was always some sort of city construction or city repair work being done on the streets this time of year, no native Angelinos would bat much of an eye at this.

Crawford and Kowalski had agreed to do what they were now doing simply because of how much money they would be paid when it was all over. They were close friends and they both needed the twenty grand they were promised. Crawford was being sued by a lady whose cat he'd run over with his UPS van and Kowalski had a shit load of legal bills and fines to pay after recently receiving his second DUI charge.

Crawford had been asked to take part in this job by a friend of his who had recently retired from the D.E.A. and gone to work in Iraq for a time as a Private Military Contractor. All that was needed was for Crawford to find one other truck driver who could come on board and perform a few "easy tasks." They would be paid handsomely to simply park the phony delivery vans in the arranged spots and punch some big red buttons on a detonator wired to something in the back of the vans. Each one was told not to even ask what was actually inside the huge vans they were driving. Both men had complied with the instructions. An advance of ten thousand dollars had already been deposited into their accounts and this made them want to work even harder to complete the last phase of their tasks. These transfers were done in successive increments ranging from no more than twenty five hundred to three thousand at a time. The rationale for this was simple: any money transfers or deposits amounting to five thousand or more had to be reported to the Securities and Exchange Commission. This fact was certainly not lost on the dark haired man who'd hired them.

Tracking transfers well below five thousand dollars would be an extremely difficult task due to the sheer volume of transactions that would have to be found, pulled up and searched.

Crawford took one last look in his friend's direction and looked down at his watch: 7:12am. Now all they had to do was listen for the signal over their Motorola Walkie Talkies so they could punch the detonators and walk fast up to West Sixth Street where they were supposed to get picked up and paid the rest of the money. He looked down at the ridiculously large red button. It looked jerry rigged to say the least.

"Guess they didn't want our dumb asses to fuck it up and push the wrong one," he said to himself.

Five blocks to the West in the Barnes and Noble parking lot off Fairfax and Third, former U.S. Army Unmanned Aerial Vehicle operators Sam Burchfield and David Taylor sat quietly inside the back of a black Ford van. They tensed up a little as their fingers prepared to fly over the keyboards and joysticks of the LCD terminals that were wired into the still experimental EX-45 Remote Weapons Platforms that were hidden in the backs of the two delivery vans. These portable, state of the art weapons stations were specifically designed to be remote controlled and operated by Sailors or Marines from a relatively long and safe distance. Each model was built to mount a slightly modified version of the M2HB Browning Fifty Caliber Heavy Machine Gun. In the case of the model emplaced inside Kowalski's van next to the Coffee Leaf, modifications had been made to allow it to mount a MK-19 Forty Millimeter automatic grenade launcher.

The M2HB in Crawford's van was loaded with a belt of red tipped M20 rounds which were designed to combine both a light armor piercing capability as well as an incendiary effect. As for the MK-19 inside Kowalski's van, the first part of its fifty round belt was comprised of fifteen High Explosive Dual Purpose munitions whose inverted cone shaped charge gave it both an armor piercing capability as well as an effective fragmentation effect. The rest of its fifty-round belt consisted of High Explosive anti-personnel rounds.

Burchfield and Taylor knew these weapon systems, as well as the EX-45s they were mounted to, inside and out. In fact, both men had operated test models only two years ago at the Aberdeen proving ground in Maryland while still on active duty. They both did what they could to contain their excitement and tension, be it fidgeting or taking deep breaths. Each one waited in silence while gazing at the view provided by the high definition gun camera mounted to each platform. Soon, the view would be filled with the light of morning.

Far to the east, at the intersection of Wilshire and Oxford, the Contractor sat comfortably inside the white Pontiac Sunfire parked next to the CVS Pharmacy building. If someone who had seen him last night saw him this morning, they wouldn't be able to recognize him with blonde hair coloring, colored contacts, and a fake goatee. He calmly listened to the Los Angeles Police Department's message traffic over the police and emergency band scanner he'd bought at Radio Shack. So far, nothing much seemed to be going on nearby but that would soon change and it was he who would personally make sure of it.

A little further down on South Serrano Avenue, Mike Sisler, a former undercover narcotics officer and retired member of the D.E.A's Clandestine Laboratory Enforcement Teams, did his best to act like the homeless bum he was dressed as. While pushing his rickety junk cart a few feet further, he watched as Abdallah Khan's black Hummer H3 Limousine slowly cruised by in the right hand lane. Sisler scratched his crotch and pretended to talk to himself while carefully speaking into the microphone concealed in his whiskey bottle.

"Veronica, Veronica," he said.

The word "Veronica" was the warning order for the truck drivers and the two operators off Fairfax and Third. The light at Wilshire and Western turned red and Khan's limousine came to a halt with only one hitch: there was a red Ford Mustang right in front of it. Well, at least they had a halfway decent contingency plan for something like this and it looked like Sisler's other partner was already on it.

Former Army infantryman and professional truck driver, Jack Hartman, had been closely following Abdallah Khan's limousine in a stolen Mack truck ever since it crossed South Vermont Avenue. Wasting no time, he backed up as far as he could, threw the semi back into gear, literally ramming into the rear of the stretched out Hummer H3. The impact crushed the rear bumper and viciously launched the limo's front end into the rear of the Mustang and pushed it halfway out into the intersection. A split second later, Hartman was leaping out of the truck to escape the line of fire.

A Mercury Mountaineer grinded to a halt a few feet away from the Mustang as Mike Sisler finally gave the execution code: "Rats in the sewer, rats in the sewer!"

No sooner had the second phrase left his mouth, than Crawford and Kowalski punched the detonator switches in between their front seats, setting off four strands of Det-Cord wrapped around the thin, flimsy, jerry-rigged chains that were holding each van's almost paper thin rear door in place.

As the chain links were nearly vaporized, the doors came crashing down onto the pavement, giving Burchfield and Taylor completely unobstructed views of the front and side sections Khan's limo. The driver of the now fucked up Ford Mustang saw the huge barrel of the MK-19 pointed right at him and slammed on the accelerator before jerking to the right onto North Western Avenue.

Inside the Ford van near Barnes and Noble, Sam Burchfield quickly moved the joystick on his remote so that the crosshairs of the MK-19 gun camera were centered on the hood of the H3 limousine. He pressed the firing button and Dave Taylor followed suit.

The world seemed to explode around the pedestrians clustered all around the intersections as a stream of eight High Explosive Dual Purpose grenades punched into the hood and grill of the Hummer limousine. The explosions bored through and blasted apart the insides of the engine block, blowing red hot shrapnel into the undercarriage and out onto the pavement underneath it. Divots of concrete shot out on either side as the last two 40mm rounds detonated further up in the engine block, blasting shards of Flak through the dashboard and literally eviscerating the face and upper body of Khan's driver.

Almost simultaneously, Dave Taylor fired off the Fifty Cal, expertly moving the joystick and the crosshairs around from the middle of the vehicle all the way to the rear and back again.

A constant, hellacious line of high caliber death was poured out in a tracer punctuated stream as the M8 rounds punched straight through the limousine's doors, frame, interior, chairs and windows. The exterior looked as if it was literally being blown apart by an invisible, exploding can opener as metal collapsed in on itself while glass shattered and jagged blossoms of eviscerated metal seemed to be swallowing Khan's vehicle like a hyper-active case of metallic blisters.

The rounds that punched through the doors either bored into the bodies inside, ripping them apart like exploding, bloody rag dolls as they tumbled through or penetrating all the way and exiting the other side. Those that kept going but had their trajectory altered by the impacts shot through the Lupus Restaurant and ricocheted all over the exterior of the Liltern theater, tearing jagged chunks of puke green stone out of the structure and raining it down on panicked bystanders.

Inside the Theatric Makeup School at the Liltern's base, two young women and one transvestite were hit by three of the stray fifty caliber rounds. Both women were hit in the chest and stomach from different angles, ripping apart their vital organs. They were dead soon after they hit the floor. The transvestite was unlucky enough to catch a round that went through one of the limousine's windows. It hit him straight through the mouth, nearly exploding his entire head as the impact spun him around and slammed him down onto the floor.

Inside the limousine, Abdallah Khan cowered on the floor beneath one of the leather couch seats. Two of his bodyguards were dead and hunks of their blood and viscera had splattered all over him right before his sexy, svelte call girl had two of her limbs torn to shreds and ripped off following some of the grenade shrapnel which had mutilated her scalp. Two of the fifty caliber rounds that had bored through the sides had then blasted into her lower body and now her mashed intestines were spilled out all over the floor, all over him.

Before he could cower any further, Khan's legs were smashed apart by two separate rounds and his entire left arm was completely ripped off at the shoulder by one that hit him squarely after punching through one of the doors. Only he and his fourth bodyguard were still alive. They both screamed like hysterical women, knowing they were going to die, terrified and alone in a bursting cauldron of body-crushing bullets, ragged shards of metal and exploding body parts.

The High Explosive Anti-Personnel rounds from the MK-19 sailed through the now nonexistent windshield straight into the vehicle's spacious interior where they hit or bounced around until they exploded. Khan and his bodyguard were both vivisected by the grenade's fragmentation blasts until their bodies were turned into nothing more than scattered, shrapnel infused clumps of burnt organs and flesh mixed with barbequed, smashed pieces of bones. The limousine's fuel lines were ignited only a split second before Khan passed from this world into the infernal regions.

Mass chaos and pandemonium carried the day around the ambushed vehicle, with cars and SUVs running into one another as their drivers panicked and tried to flee. Dozens of pedestrians ran this way and that like bleating sheep running from a pack of hungry Wolves. Still, the fifty cal kept firing and the MK-19 kept on pumping grenades into what had now become Abdallah Khan's exploding coffin.

Taylor and Burchfield calmly fired off a few more of their weapon's rounds before stopping and remote detonating the C-4 explosive charges placed around and under each platform.

The two white delivery vans exploded, scorching and severely wounding a number of bystanders that hadn't quite managed to get far enough away from the action. The combination of hot, flying shrapnel and a massive concussion wave tore apart and smashed the escalators by the Wilshire/ Western subway exit, bringing the makeshift pavilion crashing to the ground.

Burchfield and Taylor had no idea just how close they were to their last seconds on earth.

From where the Contractor was posted, the exploding vans sounded like a massive *karrummpf* sound. This reminded him about how certain loose ends were to be tied up.

The undercarriage of the van that Burchfield and Taylor *had* been working in was wired with C-4 charges primed to detonate as soon as they shut off just one of the EX-45 remote control stations. The mini-van parked up near the Wilshire intersection with West Fifth Street, which was supposed to be picked up by Kowalski and Crawford, had an explosives package in the undercarriage that was primed with a strand of Det cord wired into the starter motor. When the ignition was turned on, it was "curtains" for the truck drivers. The exact same was true for Hartman and Sisler's getaway truck that had been parked near West Seventh, south of the Koreatown McDonalds near Ingraham street. Another explosion echoed in the distance. Two more loose ends had been tied up. The Contractor's car would detonate a few minutes after he left it.

It was time to go.

He stepped out of the car after wiping down everything he'd touched and decided it was best to play monkey-see-monkey-do with the crush of fleeing civilians running up Oxford Avenue while screaming about another 9-11.

The Contractor's escape vehicle, a white Mitsubishi Eclipse, was parked and waiting near the intersection of Oxford and West Fourth Street. He stayed with the fleeing crowd before breaking off and running to it. In the process, he failed to take notice of the red Chrysler van parked a good ways down on the opposite side of the street.

Inside the red van, former French Foreign Legion sniper Jacques Rodin adjusted his body as he leaned into the stock of his Remington 700 bolt action rifle in .300 Winchester Magnum. He reached forward towards the rear door and pressed a button, holding it until the window had descended about halfway, just below the bottom of the American Armament Corporation silencer on the end of his barrel. He only knew what his target looked like and precisely where he would be at what time. As for who his target really was, well, he wasn't getting paid to ask *those* kinds of questions now, was he?

Jacques Rodin pulled the rifle's stock tight into his shoulder and adjusted the angle on the elevated shooting rest he'd put together. He aligned the crosshairs of the 3-9X variable on the chest of the blonde man with the goatee, pulling the rifle in a little tighter and filling his lungs with a deep breath. He started letting his breath out as he slowly squeezed the trigger. As he had planned, the recoil and the stock bucking into his shoulder came as a surprise to him. As always he did not anticipate the recoil like an amateur would have done.

His target stopped cold turkey and dropped dead in his tracks, his heart and chest ruptured by the high velocity, thirty-caliber bullet. Rodin wasted no time at all in jumping into the van's front seat and speeding off towards West Third Street and South Harvard Boulevard where he ditched the van after squirting lighter fluid all over the interior as well as the rifle. The timer on the charge of Semtex was set for only ten minutes.

Five minutes later, he hailed a cab and instructed the driver to take him to the Landmark Aviation terminal at LAX. The driver complied and roughly forty-five minutes later, he paid the fare and was admitted into the private aircraft area where he boarded a Gulfstream business jet. Minutes after he was welcomed aboard by an imposing man, whose background was clearly military, the plane took off and soon it was flying over the Sierra Nevada mountain range. Rodin made himself comfortable as he sat down in one of the plush leather chairs on the starboard side. If only his other clients would have shown such generosity.

It was as the plane was sailing high over the Las Vegas area that Jacques Rodin's gut instinct began telling him that something was wrong. He didn't have to wait long to see what it was.

The man who had welcomed him aboard was a former Marine Sergeant and infantry squad leader turned Hitman named J.T. Sleight, who was on the plane as a direct representative of the men who had hired both Rodin and the Contractor.

Sleight wasted no time in withdrawing a silencer suppressed 9mm Makarov from inside his sport coat and taking aim at his target's head. Jacques Rodin's first reaction was shock and then utter comprehension as four hollow points bored through his forehead and ripped through his brain.

J.T. Sleight had no idea why his current client wanted this man dead and quite frankly, he didn't care. He had completed his task and soon he would meet with his uncle, a private detective from Houston to pick up his payment.

Six hours later, inside his apartment in Geneva Switzerland, former C.I.A. Case Officer Bill Carpenter clinked his wine glass against the one held by his new friend and colleague, a powerful Swiss banker named Johann Von Braun. Some years ago, Herr Braun's daughter was blown apart in the infamous Bali nightclub bombing. The fact that Abdallah Khan had helped fund the Southeast Asian cell responsible for the massacre was never made public by American intelligence for one key reason: Khan was a distant relative of a Saudi Prince with connections to the family of America's current President. This had incensed Carpenter to no end and after coming to Switzerland and getting to know Von Braun, he had soon learned about his daughter's fate in Bali.

A deal had been struck and a scheme had been hatched between the two men, both of whom were quite thorough in all that they did. Although Carpenter and Von Braun disagreed on many issues, one thing they quickly agreed on was this: Qatari billionaires who fund Islamic terrorists are every bit as dangerous as loose ends.

THE END

ANGEL OF THE CITY

7:45 pm. Houston, Texas. Richmond Avenue. Greenway Plaza. The Israeli Consulate.

Colonel David Shamir of the Israeli Mossad leaned back in his leather office chair, allowing the last swig of coffee to wash down his throat before scanning back over the dossier that had been sent to him from Tel Aviv over a month ago. The pudgy face of the Arab man inside it appeared somewhat arrogant, with a smug smile indicative of an extremely wealthy, privileged upbringing of the sort that would endow someone with a sense of superiority and entitlement. On the surface, the rotund and obese Prince Ali Saud appeared to be just another pampered blood member of the Saudi Royal family, but in fact, like many others of his ilk, he regularly engaged in activities that gave direct support to Islamic terrorist groups. Within the last year, Prince Ali Saud had transferred millions of American dollars out of his own accounts and into those of financiers working for Hezbollah, Al-Qaida and Hamas, the brutal Palestinian terrorist organization whose suicide bombers had slaughtered so many Israelis in recent years. In fact, Prince Saud had even promised the families of successful suicide bombers enough money to allow them to live comfortably for the rest of their lives since their deceased relatives had killed so many infidels and thus had become "martyrs." Colonel Shamir shivered with hatred every time he heard *that* term used to describe such evil murderers who had butchered so many of his countrymen. That hatred began to fade away when David Shamir thought of what lay in store for Ali Saud later tonight.

When Mossad headquarters in Tel Aviv had sent him Ali Saud's dossier they had been very clear about what they wanted Shamir to do with all of the detailed surveillance information: kill the Saudi prince in such a way as to send another strong message to Israel's enemies and leave no evidence trail that could be traced directly back to the Mossad. Such a task was "old hat" for a man like Shamir and after some thinking he decided to set up a meeting with a "cutout" from a locally based Private Security Firm known as Mercury Securities. Owned and operated by retired members of America's military and intelligence communities, Mercury Securities often hired and recruited ex-Special Forces types from around the world to do some of the U.S. government's dirty work in places like Central America and Afghanistan. The Firm's more public activities such as the contract work they did for local Law Enforcement agencies or the state of the art alarm systems they designed are what attracted most of the public's attention. Only a few investigative journalists had ever attempted to search beyond the Company's shiny veneer. Mercury Securities had a reputation for protecting their client's confidentiality and finding the right man to get the job done, although in this case it wouldn't be a man. That was all the ex-military "cutout" would tell Shamir after their third private meeting, long after the information on when the Prince would be back in Houston had changed hands. After closing and locking up the remains of the intelligence files on his desk, David Shamir walked downstairs and strolled out into the moist night air to have a smoke.

After lighting up and taking a pull on his cigarette, he looked out above Richmond Avenue towards the pleasure gratifying regions of the city's popular west side. A smile appeared on Shamir's face as he pondered what horrors were awaiting Prince Ali Saud, what with his weakness for pretty American women. If only he could've imagined what they would be.

7:56 pm. Westheimer Road near Beltway 8.

Prince Ali Saud leaned back and stretched out his legs before grabbing a crystal wine glass from the black limousine's cooler and pouring himself a shot of scotch on the rocks, sipping it conservatively so as to savor the taste. Already, his current trip to Houston to meet with one of his cousins who worked as a professor of Arab studies at the University of St. Thomas was shaping up to be better than he had planned. After showering and unwinding in the Presidential Suite of the Adam's Mark hotel, Ali Saud had looked down at the floor near the doorway to find that someone had walked by and slipped a glossy business card under the door and into his room. He had made a mental note to tell his two bodyguard's Yasir Hossein and Tariq Salim, to get off their lazy asses in the suite's next door room, but thought better of it when he read what was printed on the card. Set in between a picture of red roses and the outline of a woman's lacy panties, were the words:

> *"Looking For a Hot Night of Kinky, Carnal Pleasures, call Tiffany.*
>
> *Will Gadly Do S&M. Very Discreet. Satisfaction Guaranteed." 281-498-7179.*

Perhaps it was a blessing from Allah or even a present from a relative. Either way, whoever had shoved that card under the door definitely knew what *he* liked. When Ali called the phone number on the card, the sweet, silky smooth, seductive voice that answered sounded as if it had been waiting all night long just for him. When he asked if she would be willing to tie him up and get abusive when they copulated, she just said "Oh Baby, we can do whatever you want," a barely audible moan escaping her lips afterward.

Ali had made an appointment for 8:45 pm. the same night at the Tiara Plaza Hotel off the Northwest Freeway. Tiffany would be waiting for him in room 317. All Ali had to do was knock and walk in to pay the six hundred dollars for the hour and a half they had agreed on. As the sleek, black limousine cruised east on Westheimer towards the 610 Loop, Ali Saud nodded at his second bodyguard, Tariq Salim, who in turn rapped on the window that separated the driver's compartment from the rest of the vehicle. Yasir Hossein took his cue and sped up, knowing just how anxious his boss could get when it came to fucking these *infidel* women.

Two cars behind Saud's Limousine, retired Marine and ex-Houston Cop Art Smithson applied more pressure on the Honda Accord's accelerator in order to keep pace with his surveillance Mark. So far, that racy, business card he had slipped under the Hotel room's door had done the trick and caught Saud's perverted interest. As he cruised past Hillcroft, Smithson glanced up and caught sight of the powerful, rotating saber of light emanating from the top of the monolithic Williams Tower. At this distance the light beam's non-stop, rotational tolling was almost hypnotic, as if it could keep turning around and around, totally oblivious to whatever dangerous or horrific events transpired in the streets and freeways below. Tonight, that would be proven to be especially true as the infamous searchlight spun itself around well into the early hours of the morning.

8:00 pm. 12801 Northwest Freeway. The Tiara Plaza Hotel.

This particular *infidel* woman was named Breena Stone, not Tiffany. No high dollar Call Girl/Escort ever used her *real* name, but the men could certainly think that if they wanted to. Such a notion was just one of the many illusions she and others permitted their clients to have. They made their *experience* together even more pleasurable and helped to produce repeat customers.

Breena Stone was just one of many hundreds of Independent female Escorts who primarily worked out of the west and northwest sides of the city. The occasional contract killing, like her work as an Escort, was a side job that complemented her day job as a Fitness Instructor at the Bally's Total Fitness on Highway 290 where she stayed in fantastic shape and kept her slender, shapely body toned to near perfection. Breena Stone was thirty years old but hardly looked a day over twenty-seven. Many a male customer had tripped or dropped a set of weights on the floor while watching her walk by in either a leotard after an aerobics class or a bikini on her way back from the pool. She loved it when they did that.

She had been working out of the Tiara Plaza Hotel for some time now and the various "hush-hush" monetary "arrangements" she had made with the Hotel manager, a fat, lonesome, bald guy named Tom Perkins, permitted her to simply walk in through the back door and go straight up to her continually reserved room, thereby avoiding the public front lobby and its numerous security cameras. An occasional free blowjob went a long way with a horny, lonely man like Tom. As she entered through the west entrance and strolled down the hallway, Breena Stone looked every bit the part of a pixie faced, large breasted, super seductive heartbreaker with an erection igniting, semen launching figure and a vivacious mane of long, thick, silky chestnut-colored hair conditioned to an almost perfect shine that seemed to sparkle under the hallway lights. Whenever she removed her sunglasses, her eyes became luminescent sapphires that could lock onto a man's pupils with all the focused intensity of a Helium-Argon laser, burning a path straight to his balls and adrenal glands.

Even though she currently wore nothing but a sweatshirt and sweatpants, Breena Stone still moved with the Jaguar-like grace of a lust lioness on the prowl for a lusty mate as she stepped into the elevator and pushed the button for the eighth floor. With her gym bag already filled to capacity, she couldn't wait until she got to her room where she could toss it on the bed and really get to work.

Once inside the room, Breena Stone closed the room's curtains, dumped the contents of her heavy gym bag onto the bedspread and turned to face the mirror where she began to strip off her sweats, casually slipping out of them with all the grace of a mythical Greek goddess moving through the Heavens. She kicked the top and bottom of her jogging suit to the other side of the room, pulling her luscious hair up above her shoulders and flashing a mischievous smile at the mirror, admiring the reflection of her fully nude figure, once again feeling satisfied with all the work it took to maintain her toned thighs, tight stomach and pert breasts that had undergone mild enhancement surgery three years ago. Knowing that she didn't have that much time left to get ready, she pinned up the rest of her hair with bobby pins and grabbed a pair of micro scissors and a tiny, electric razor out of her purse and set to work trimming up the tiny strip of dark brown pubic hair above her vulva, the stubble shorn, mildly waxed region surrounding the part of her body that she had used, along with her mouth, to give so many men so much pleasure over the past few years. Once she was done shearing up the tiny, "landing strip" above her pelvic region, she gently stroked her sex, her fingers gliding into the fleshy wetness spreading outward and smiled again, feeling every bit the part of the penultimate seductress. She knew that the extra hours of the more private workouts she did at home in the way of squats and timed masturbation with sex toys had so seriously strengthened the inner muscles around her vagina that she could probably coax an orgasm out of an Egyptian Mummy. Reaching back into the side pocket of her purse, Breena Stone removed a small, plastic capsule shaped like a Tampon and deftly inserted it into her vaginal canal, quickly squeezing her legs back together to secure it in place. What was inside the long, plastic capsule would be the most vital tool in the arsenal that she would need to complete the actual job that she had been contracted to do.

After placing the scissors and razor back into her purse, Breena began to slip on two pieces of shiny black lingerie, starting with the thong panty. She smoothly spread her legs as she brought the thong high up into the middle of her rear and cinched it up around her hips, stretching her legs further apart as the crotch of the panty fully encased her womanhood. The sensuous feel of the silk against her folds of skin only mildly aroused her as she placed her supple breasts in the lacy bra and swiftly snapped it into place in between her shoulder blades. She closed her legs and gently ran her hands down the length of her stomach and thighs before wrapping her legs in a pair of dark black, silk stockings which were secured in place to the waistline of her panty with dark, ruffled clips. Reaching back into the gym bag, she pulled out a bright red, velvet miniskirt and squeezed her gorgeous figure into it, pulling the bottom down as far as it would go, leaving only about four inches of material between the tops of her quadriceps and hips. The mere sight of Breena Stone's figure wrapped up in a mini-skirt tight enough to be used as a spandex pant leg for an anorexic Ethiopian would've stopped any man dead in his tracks, making him stare at something he would give anything to have. She checked through the contents of her gym bag one last time, glancing at the black leather whips and the ball gag before settling on the nylon ropes and the waist harness. The latter devices would serve dual purposes tonight, as would her feminine wiles.

Breena Stone still knew that it was her looks that would end up being the most powerful weapon in regards to setting Ali Saud up for his demise, just as much as she and other women in her profession knew, that a more appropriate title for Helen of Troy would've been "the tight-body pussy that lured thousands of men to their deaths." She removed the bobby pins from her hair, letting it cascade over her shoulders like dark, homespun gold shimmering over cream colored, marble flooring and simply waited, thinking not only of the man to be killed, but of the father she was never able to grow up with.

After Yasir Hossein parked the limousine catty corner from the Hotel's main entrance, Prince Ali Saud squeezed his fat, robed figure out of the rear door and quickly walked inside with Tariq Salim in tow. The corpulent Saudi Prince's mind was focused only on using another woman for gratification, making him just as oblivious to the roar of traffic and the loud music blaring out of Joe's Crab Shack across the freeway as he was to the fact that he was being watched. This of course, was perfectly fine with Art Smithson, who had just pulled in and parked on the other side of the parking lot facing in the direction of Logan's Roadhouse.

As the Prince and his rough looking bodyguard exited the elevator on the third floor they turned left and walked up to room 317. Saud knocked heavily on the door until he heard footsteps on the other side and seconds later, the sound of a latch being disengaged. As the door opened and Breena Stone smiled, both men felt a familiar rush of blood in their loins. Earlier, Ali had asked Tariq what he thought about the two of them going into the room and raping the "sluttish infidel woman" as Hossein had referred to her. Tariq made it clear that this was a bad idea since if she screamed someone might call the police which might lead to the Prince being shot, since these Texas "Cowboy" cops had a reputation for being rough on sex offenders and not giving a damn about whether a crime perpetrator had tons of money, especially if that "perp" was Middle Eastern. Tariq might be having second thoughts now, but no matter, he would get to "search" her to make sure she had no dangerous weapons that could be used, other than those needed for the S&M session they'd agreed upon. Ali pushed his way in with Tariq and shut the door, putting his hands up as a bewildered look crossed Breena's face.

"Do not worry, Tiffany, this man, Tariq is my bodyguard. He is simply here to search you very quickly," chirped Saud.

"Sweetie, that wasn't part of the deal. It's not really necessary," responded Breena as she innocently batted her long eyelashes at him.

"Please, Ms. Tiffany, I am an important man, with dangerous enemies, many of whom are Zionists lapdogs for Israel. It will only take a few seconds, then I make my bodyguard go away."

Breena finally relented and maintained an air of grace as Tariq ran his hands up and down her body, occasionally squeezing on areas far too close for comfort to her some of her more intimate regions, probably enjoying himself immensely.

"This fucking sand pig of a client is going to pay for having his dog grope me," she thought to herself.

After finishing the body search, Tariq rummaged through her belongings. After he was satisfied that there was nothing to be found but nylon ropes, a digital camera, whips, something that looked like a waist harness of some sort and a ball gag, Tariq nodded at his boss and left the room. Ali Saud handed over the cash in advance as he had agreed to do and watched as the infidel whore bent over and stuffed it in her purse. Breena Stone then re-locked the door before turning to her soon to be deceased "client" with a lascivious smile on her face as she ran her hands over his chest and down towards the middle of his groin, feeling him harden in her gentle grasp. Prince Saud gasped and, worrying about his usual problem with premature ejaculation, asked if they could take off all their clothes and move to the bed.

"Sure thing Baby, just lie down and get naked while I get more comfortable," intoned Breena.

Ali Saud did as he was told, the captivating quality of the woman's beauty and feminine charm nearly hypnotizing him as he slipped out of his robes and lay down naked. As she slipped out of the mini-skirt, Breena watched with perfectly disguised revulsion as the Prince's erection became more pronounced against his bulbous belly. She un-wound the nylon ropes and glided over Ali, tying his wrists to the bedposts and rubbing her breasts over his chest, feeling the increasing rapidity of his breath as sweat began to ooze from his fatty flesh.

"Thank God I got his hands tied up before he asked if he could grab my tits or my pussy," she thought to herself as she remembered that these guys were supposed to wipe their assholes with one of their hands. Breena ran her tongue over his lips before pushing the ball gag into his mouth and locking it in place behind his head. The kinky S&M session Ali Saud had paid for was about to end up being much rougher than he could've ever imagined in his worst nightmares. Breena Stone smiled at him as she began cracking the two leather whips. Ali Saud noticed that before his whore for the night had grabbed the whips, she had slipped on some rubber latex gloves and then a black leather pair over those. Without any show of emotion, she pulled a digital camera from her gym bag and took three pictures of Ali Saud, strapped down in a remarkably embarrassing position. Saud became shocked and puzzled at this.

After putting the camera back in her duffle bag, Breena moved forward and then straddled Ali's crotch, allowing him to run up against the crotch of her panties. She dropped the whips and slid the middle of her black panty away from her crotch and dug fingers into her vaginal canal, quickly removing the thin plastic capsule she had placed there earlier. Saud wondered what in the name of Allah the *infidel* whore had just pulled out of her sex organs. Suddenly, the seductive smile vanished from her face as a a glare of deep, vicious hate filled her eyes.

"I better kill this fucker quick before he cums all over me and I have to take an alcohol bath," she whispered to herself as she ripped the top of the capsule off, revealing a thin, razor sharp, scalpel shaped knife with a serrated edge that glistened in the dim light of the scented candles she had placed on the nightstand. Breena moved further up on Ali's stomach to put some distance between her sex and his prick, rocking back and forth grunting, moaning and emitting almost every erotic sound a young woman could make while in the throes of intense sexual passion.

Breena clamped her left hand down hard on the ball gag in the Prince's mouth as she shoved the knife all the way through the flesh, fat and muscle covering his sternum and solar plexus, blood squirting out around the weapon's hilt. Ali's entire body stiffened as he bit deeper into the rubber of the ball gag. She intensified her moans and cries while pushing downward on the knife, drawing it all the way down through the Saudi Prince's stomach in the direction of his groin area. She kept pace with it in order to avoid the blood flow while literally slicing the belly open from chest to crotch, opening him up like a ripe melon being cut open in the summer air. Ali Saud's insides began to slowly pour out of his open belly as he bit and tore even deeper in the ball gag, literally tearing his teeth out of their gums in agony and pain, unable to let out anything resembling a scream. After the disembowelment permitted his intestines to uncoil in a steaming pile near his hips, Breena Stone placed a large white towel over Saud's throat and deftly sliced open his carotid artery, her sex moistening the "V" of her panties as she was filled with the perverse excitement of making him bleed to death, the bright terrycloth almost instantly changing into a dark, crimson color. Outside, Tariq Salim figured his boss was having just another grand old time getting fucked and beaten at the same time by a western woman.

"Merciful Allah, if only I should be so lucky," he thought to himself.

Knowing that she didn't have too much time left, Breena stuffed her miniskirt, purse and whips back into her gym bag and slipped back into her jogging suit before grabbing the digital camera and snapping off three more shots of Prince Ali Saud's bleeding, eviscerated body. She stuffed the camera back into her gym bag before slipping on a pair of welder's gloves to prevent "ropeburn" and then moving about the room with a washcloth, wiping down everything she could remember touching. She quickly went to untie Saud's wrists, yanking away on the long strands of nylon rope after pulling the rappelling harness out of her gym bag and skillfully slinging both its straps over her shoulders like a backpack. After tying a series of tight knots around the leg of the bed and running the other two nylon rope strands through the waist harness, she opened up the curtains and the room's window and threw the loose ends of rope outside and down to the ground, knowing that the lights below that usually shine up to illuminate this part of the hotel, which didn't face the freeway, would've already been shot out with a pellet rifle belonging to the man from Mercury Securities that she had been working with.

Breena carefully slid her lower body out of the window, using her feet to find footing on the wall and then kicking herself away from it and loosening her grip on the rope twice in a row. Once she felt her heels touching the bushes, Breena simply let go, hit the ground, pulled the rest of the rope back through the harness before unlocking its hasps and running to her car. After starting the car and revving up its engine, she cruised out of the parking lot and merged onto the southbound lanes of the Northwest Freeway, on her way to deliver the embarrassing pictures of Prince Ali Saud to a predetermined location where they would be picked up by the man who had always looked out for her, the man who she had worked with in recent years who would see that she was well taken care of after this hit. The digital pictures would then be taken to an investigative reporter who worked for the Houston Post newspaper and eventually, some "muck raking" internet journalists as well. She smiled as she drove into the heart of the city to pick up her belongings and get ready to move elsewhere to a new identity and a new life. This time, her smile only faded halfway when she thought about her father, dying in a far off land when she was so young.

One week later.

Sitting in the parking lot of the Randall's Supermarket on Westheimer and Gessner, Art Smithson cracked a mischievous smile as he glanced down at the recent edition of the Houston Post, chuckling to himself while gazing upon some of the mildly censored yet still embarrassing, front page pictures of Ali Saud tied to a bed in bondage regalia. The Saudi Royal Family would be reeling from this incident for years to come. He felt just as satisfied knowing that he and Mercury Securities gave the Israelis their money's worth as he did about getting Breena out of Houston with a shit load of cash and a new life in another city. It was something she deserved more than almost any woman he had ever known. As he set his coffee down in the cup holder, Smithson felt overwhelmed by a sense of nostalgia which compelled him to yank out his wallet and look at a picture he had put there long ago. When he looked at it, it seemed like a dozen lifetimes since it was taken. It was a picture taken in 1983 of two young, cocky, M-16 toting Marine Corporals in Beirut Lebanon, both full of piss and vinegar and a burning desire to kick the holy hell out of every communist or rag head motherfucker on the globe. The camouflage blouse of the Marine on the left had a nametape that read **SMITHSON**, while the one on the right said **STONE**.

THE END

THE VIGILANTE

March 5th, 2011. 11:47 pm. Tijuana, Mexico.

My name is Mike Hardin, Sergeant, U.S.M.C. Retired and up until very recently I was working as a Mercenary for a firm known as Dark Skies Security. The chain of events that had led to me being where I am now, just a few miles south of the San Diego border crossing in an abandoned apartment, with a masculine looking "dyke" of a woman, bound and gagged before me and pleading for mercy after being brutally beaten and tortured, were ultimately set into motion on June twenty seventh, 2010. On that day, at 11:30 am, a total of twelve Islamic terrorists walked into four different shopping malls in San Diego, Phoenix, El Paso and Albuquerque and set off the explosives laden vests they were wearing. The motherfuckers blew themselves up and took hundreds of innocent Americans, primarily women and young children, with them.

The "suicide vests" these sub-human savages wore were similar to those used by Palestinian homicide bombers in the West Bank and each was packed with roughly 30 pounds of C-4 high explosive wrapped in thick layers of steel ball bearings, which turned the exploding terrorists into gigantic, Claymore anti-personnel mines. In some cases, the women and children who were instantly killed by the blast overpressure and the ball bearings tearing through their vital organs were the "lucky" ones. Amidst all of the hysteria that followed the constant news coverage, hundreds of pictures from all four of the destroyed malls found their way onto a few TV stations, lots of newspapers and hundreds more news websites, many of which were totally uncensored. They were often too horrible for many people to stomach, but millions of Americans still saw them.

Photographs of dozens of children and their mothers ripped apart, nearly blown in half or missing arms, legs, mouths, jaws or even faces both terrified and outraged the American public in a ways that hadn't been seen since the massacre of September 11th.

One such picture that leaked out was snapped by a curious pedestrian near the Horton Plaza Mall in downtown San Diego, barely two minutes after one of the bombers, a Saudi Arabian named Khamal Fahd, detonated his suicide vest and blew himself up about twenty feet away from the Victoria's Secret store in the middle of a crowd of Moms and kids lingering around some toy displays. The photograph captured a thirty something woman missing the lower half her right arm, a jagged maw of mutilated flesh where her right elbow used to be, running mad down the steps by the Mall's front entrance, desperately clutching her child, a girl about 4 years old. The little girl's stomach was torn open and her legs were nearly gone. I can still remember seeing that picture. I felt a sort of anger and rage unlike any I had felt in my entire adult life as a Marine and then a Mercenary. Later on, with that picture stuck in my head I even felt like going to church for the first time in over a decade just to see what it would be like to actually pray for God to take mercy on the stricken souls of His followers.

The problem is, I'm not the church-going type.

The fear and panic that followed everyone's outrage led to malls and shopping centers having to shut down for a while because no one was going to them so soon after such an attack-they were too damn scared. The damage to the economy was nothing to scoff at and initially, as could be expected, there was a massive increase in online shopping following a small economic downturn.

As the F.B.I, A.T.F. and Police Departments in the four cities that were struck began to piece things together, it became clearer what had happened. Four separate, three-man Al-Qaida cells were found to have been the perpetrators. Every single one of these worthless goddamn fuck-heads was a young, Arabic male, Islamic extremist from various Middle Eastern countries ranging from Saudi Arabia to Iraq and Syria. They had all infiltrated the United States by simply sneaking across the un-secured border with Mexico and were helped along by professional human smugglers known as "Coyotes" who are often employed by various Drug Cartels to smuggle in cocaine. When these asshole Muslims showed up with fat wads of American cash, the smugglers were only too happy to help.

As usual, a ton of hand-wringing in Washington D.C. followed the attacks. The liberal Democrats blamed the Republicans for what happened, alleging that the War in Iraq was to blame. The Republicans, along with a few of their Talk Radio mouthpieces screamed that it was strictly the fault of the "liberal media" and the Left for "undermining" the War on Terror and not supporting the President. The bureaucrats in charge of various government agencies like Homeland Security and the T.S.A. insisted that they could've stopped it if only they'd been given more money and more power.

On radio stations across the country, thousands of Americans from all walks of life screamed, hollered and cried out for more "security." Many of those who raised legitimate questions as to whether demanding more security from the bloated and historically inept Federal government was really the best way to combat a swift, amorphous enemy, were denounced as "un-patriotic."

Such denunciations remained virulent even if those stipulating other ideas had served in the military and could see that the Federal government already had a piss-poor track record when it came to actually protecting their citizens, but had a long and distinguished record when it came to abusing, robbing and molesting them, the I.R.S. and the T.S.A. being the prime examples that were often cited. Such stipulations did resonate with Americans who had suffered such abuses, but in the end it was to no avail. Anyone who pointed out that the attacks could've easily resulted from the government's un-willingness to do anything to secure the border or, God forbid, offend Mexico, were either denounced as racists by the hardcore Left or blown off by the more dedicated, "Conservative" Republican voters who wanted to support whatever the current Republican President wanted to do While ignoring any legitimate criticism or contrary suggestions being put forth by any analytically minded member of the Law Enforcement or military communities.

As had happened right after 9-11, the White House and the top ranks of government agencies were easily able to absolve themselves of any blame through a ton of professional "spin-doctoring" and the oral spewing of just the right sort of "sound-bytes," even though lower level Intelligence and Law Enforcement specialists had warned about such an attack many years ago and suggested a number of simple countermeasures, all of which were well documented. These included recruiting Servicemen and veteran Police Officers of Latin American and Hispanic descent to serve in agencies like the C.I.A. so that a vast human intelligence network could be built up south of the border. Instead, the government insisted on relying upon more "high-tech" information gathering methods which usually involved nothing but more of the same fancy communications intercept techniques or spying on innocent ordinary Americans rather than foreigners who may represent a genuine threat.

Another "street smart" suggestion was an innovative program put into play years earlier by the Miami Police Department in Florida. Rather than try to lock their city down like an actual Police State to secure every public venue, something which was clearly impossible, Miami P.D. did something that made sense and would in no way violate any citizens rights or dignity: they took SWAT cops and Vice cops and formed them into small, mobile units carrying assorted weapons and high speed body armor whose mission was to randomly pick out large public places (like malls, parks, stadiums etc) and simply show up totally un-announced to demonstrate a robust and well armed police presence whose patterns could thus never be determined by any terrorists. They carried rucksacks full of First-Aid and First Responder gear just in case of an attack and they did not grope, pat-down or even randomly search the citizens they came into contact with.

Instead, they kept their eyes peeled for anything that, in the words of Miami Police Lieutenant Jonathan Ward, looked "genuinely suspicious," and courteously greeted nearly every citizen they came into contact with. Then, they simply handed out neon flyers containing useful information on how to spot suicide bombers, search vehicles for explosives, treat injuries and how to contact any Miami-Dade Law Enforcement agencies as well as the F.B.I. This program could not only psychologically deter terrorists, since the cops grouped together at work every morning and picked locations out at random (therefore any attackers had no way of even guessing when or where the police would show up next), but make ordinary Miami citizens feel genuinely *involved* in counter-terrorism rather than simply left out, terrified and victimized, as the policies of agencies like the D.H.S. and T.S.A. had clearly done in recent years. Such a "street smart" solution, which entailed no violations of dignity or Constitutional Amendments while producing dozens of valuable intelligence tips for Law Enforcement was also cast aside by politicians, Homeland Security officials and various talking head pundits as being "too risky or too weak."

Any smart suggestion that didn't involve raping the taxpayers even more, or increasing our government's control over us domestically, were brushed aside, regardless of who stipulated them. The American people, perhaps understandably so, were just too damn emotional to listen to reason and while a lot of guys like me, felt that massive nuclear retaliation against the nations that harbored these terrorists before the attacks was justified, too many folks just accepted that this wouldn't happen since our officials were too chicken shit to actually do it.

The fact that the refusal of our own government to do anything to secure our borders was a contributing factor to these attacks taking place, was lost upon both the Republicans and Democrats. For the Democrats it was the Hispanic vote they wanted, while the Republican's corporate constituents wanted tons of cheap labor to fill the demand created when many of their offspring had become too fucking lazy and conceited to do menial tasks as teenagers like mow lawns.

Soon, the aftermath of 9-11 began to fully repeat itself and the Big Government Republicans and like-minded Democrats couldn't get enough of the opportunity to expand their power and control. Once more, the rulers of the Federal government would do all in their power to harass, intimidate and abuse the ordinary American whose taxes paid their obscene salaries while fretting over any so-called "abuses" inflicted on foreign terrorists trying to kill us.

Thus, a new Federal agency, the P.P.A., was created.

The Public Protection Agency was to be the latest branch of the Department of Homeland Security and its purpose was, in the words of the President, "to secure all public shopping facilities and any other establishments where large numbers of Americans gather for commerce and entertainment." What soon followed was an almost picture perfect repetition of America's Airport Security fiascos, only at different locations and on a larger scale. After the National Guard left their posts at shopping centers and malls, tens of thousands of P.P.A. screeners took their place, setting up narrow and restricted security checkpoints nationwide. In the rush to hire so many screeners, little or no background checking was done and hundreds, perhaps thousands, of low-life transients, scumbags and Felons were hired. The Public Protection Agency's ranks swelled even further when it was announced that intense searches of persons and their belongings would be conducted along with what one D.H.S. official called "thorough pat-downs and friskings to insure safety and security for all American consumers." God only knows how many perverts and maybe even sex offenders were hired as screeners.

It wasn't that long before some horrific news stories about P.P.A. screeners groping and strip-searching women and young girls were broadcast in a handful of cities. P.P.A. and D.H.S. officials gave the usual line of bullshit about being sorry and taking every complaint seriously and then lectured TV viewers about the need for us to sacrifice liberty for security. Soon afterwards, there were a handful of incidents in five different cities in which fathers and husbands physically assaulted a few P.P.A. screeners who had molested their wives or daughters. In one case, an obese female screener at a Phoenix, Arizona mall, cornered a young girl and forced her to expose herself by yanking up her short blue jean skirt. The girl's father belted the screener across the face and was promptly arrested for assault and battery, although the charges were later dropped by the Phoenix Police Department after interviews with some witnesses.

However, without security cameras installed at every checkpoint, few of these cases went far. A few more men and women nationwide tried to fight back against the abuses they suffered by either filing charges for robbery or sexual assault against the screeners through the Police Departments. Unfortunately, this didn't last long. As a result of news reports about some P.P.A. screeners getting the shit kicked out of them in states like Texas, Congress passed a far reaching extension of the USA Patriot Act known as *The Public Servants Protection Act Of 2011* which made it a Federal Offense to "verbally or physically assault any security screener employed by the P.P.A." To do so would result in either a 10,000 dollar fine or up to four years imprisonment. A few Republican and Democrat politicians stated that "the Act was necessary to protect the men and women in the P.P.A. who are courageously working to preserve freedom and liberty."

There were a few stubborn souls who later challenged the P.P.A. in Federal Court after they were either robbed (an MSNBC Investigates Report revealed that the dollar amounts of items stolen from consumers by P.P.A. screeners at shopping mall checkpoints in major cities numbered in the millions) or had their spouses or children molested. The Federal District Courts kept ruling in favor of the P.P.A. and finally one case, *Thompson v. P.P.A.,* reached the Supreme Court. With the aid of a large Midwestern legal firm, a Denver, Colorado, woman named Martha Thompson was challenging the legality of a recent P.P.A. edict that, along with female consumers, all children entering malls or large shopping centers be required to remove all outer garments and if necessary, undergarments and hand probing of their bodies without the presence or consent of their parent or legal guardian, if ordered to do so by a P.P.A. screener.

Such a policy was already illegal under numerous Federal and State statutes nationwide, yet it didn't seem to matter. The black-robed, Supreme Court Oligarchs ruled that such invasive body searches of females or young children were "in no way illegal or un-Constitutional, if done by a member of the same sex for the purpose of preserving national security."

The fact that numerous thieves, assorted scumbags, Amazonian lesbo-dyke bitches and Felons were hired by the P.P.A. in the post attack panic didn't seem to matter. Our Nation's highest court, whose purpose was to properly interpret and uphold the Constitution, had just codified sexual assault and child molestation of American women and children, all so we could feel safe from a bunch of foreign fucking male towel heads from the Middle East who snuck across a border that the State and Federal governments refused to secure. Of course, it wasn't much longer until politicians, P.P.A. employees, assorted Federal bureaucrats and government officials from nearly all agencies along with *their* families were exempt from any harassment by the P.P.A. The ruling that allowed this to happen was handed down by Federal judges in the case of *ACLU v D.H.S.*

The fact that these attacks and those of 9-11 were perpetrated by a bunch of crazy, Arab Islamic, male foreigners from the goddamn Middle East didn't seem to matter to anyone working at the highest levels of the State. The fact that it wasn't parents with small children, or women and young girls from Caucasian, African-American, Asian or Hispanic backgrounds that perpetrated such attacks and made up the religion and ethnicity that such murderers typically came from, obviously failed to cross the minds of any of the idiotic retards that worked in government.

Yes, to a certain extent I am advocating a sort of religious or ethnic discrimination against a foreign culture of nutcases who think that by slaughtering *infidels* (that's us if you didn't know), they can go fuck the hell out of 72 virgin girls in heaven with Allah. Hell, if nothing else, my comparison of the current asinine P.P.A. policies to those of an organization that tries to stop white male sex predators by molesting their child-age victims is quite a fine illustration of how purely illogical and fucking stupid government at all levels really is. The fact that the attacks represented a failure on the part of American government at all levels, civilian and military, didn't seem to matter either.

It wasn't long before my ex-wife, Tammy, and my already blossoming fourteen-year-old daughter, Angela (both of whom I love dearly) were subjected to "random" molestation by the P.P.A. in San Diego.

The two of them were going to do Christmas shopping at the Horton Plaza Mall near Broadway Circle in downtown. After emptying their pockets and proceeding through the main security checkpoint next to Long's drugstore, a large bull dyke P.P.A. screener with a high and tight, whitewall haircut cornered Tammy while swinging a metal detector wand like a baseball bat and said; "Hey there, sweetheart, you've been selected for a random, secondary screening, so grab the little one and come here!"

My ex-wife, a pretty lady whose looks must've been what attracted the screener's attention, felt confused and said; "but wait, I didn't set off the metal detector and I'm like, obviously not carrying any illegal stuff like guns or knives..."

"I don't give a fuck, honey pie, get your ass in gear, grab your daughter and hustle your ass into the private screening room, right fucking now!" yelled the screener, now red faced and agitated.

"But, I don't understand," pleaded Tammy, now getting scared.

"Mom, I'm scared, let's just do what she says and maybe we'll be ok," pleaded Angela as she clutched her little pink purse in trepidation (she often does this when she gets scared).

"Enough a' this shit, I'm about to call out a Threat Alert if you and your little sweet tart don't fucking move it woman!" the screener warned.

Finally, Tammy began walking towards the window-less secondary screening room next to the Discovery Channel store and before she could turn around and tell Angela to wait outside and that everything was going to be ok, the P.P.A. dyke yelled, "Oh hell no, little missy, she's coming too," and with that, both Tammy and Angela were pushed into the dreaded secondary screening room. Once inside, the dyke bitch along with three overweight, nasty looking male P.P.A. screeners cornered them inside a more isolated area of the room and proceeded to repeatedly go over them with the metal detecting wands, taking great pains to grope and squeeze any area that caused the wand to beep, including Tammy and Angela's breasts and vaginal areas. Tammy recently had breast surgery to remove a tumor and her surgical staples kept setting off the wand. After the bull dyke had yanked open Tammy's staples and made her cry out in agony, the initial hand search stopped. Soon, Angela was left curled up on the floor in the fetal position after the bull dyke yanked up on her skirt, exposing her before she and two of the male screeners moved in and aggressively probed her private areas with their gloved hands and then saying, "ok, she's clean" before smugly stating that in a secondary screening it was required that such intensive body searches be performed to check for explosives. When Tammy started threatening to scream for help or call the Police, the incredibly obese P.P.A. Supervisor who was watching with his hands folded, simply smiled and said: "This is for national security lady and if you keep screaming and tryin' to fight us, we'll have ya' slapped with a ten thousand dollar fine and toss you and your child in jail together for a fuckin' Federal Offense! You either submit or go to jail and the Supreme Court says it's gotta be that way!"

"Ya' know, Simon, I think she's resistin' 'cause she's got somethin' to hide, like maybe some explosives or a knife to kill somebody with," intoned the dyke screener.

The fat ass of a supervisor agreed and directed the screeners to force Tammy to strip to her undergarments and spread eagle. When the dyke reached for Tammy's crotch, her hand got slapped away twice. This would quickly lead to something worse. The dyke and her Supervisor smiled at each other as they all crowded around Tammy, spewing out a new set of terse instructions and warning again that if she failed to comply, both she and Angela would be carted off to prison for, as the Screener Protection and Patriot Act extension laws now say, "failing to comply with a screener's request and/or in any way interfering with an official P.P.A. security screening."

After struggling to keep herself from bursting into tears, Tammy, far more terrified of what would happen to Angela if she didn't do as she was ordered, sucked it up and complied with the both the dyke and the Supervisor's commands, removing her panties at the top of a nearby stairwell, opening her legs and duck walking down the stairs to see if any "prohibited items" fell out[6]. After this disgusting humiliation, the pudgy asshole Supervisor gallantly told Tammy that she and Angela could put their clothes on and go about their business and that she should remember that "security is everyone's responsibility." They also warned her that trying to file charges against them would do no good even with the incident recorded on security tapes since the courts had ruled that P.P.A. screeners could not be charged for anything done "while in the course of their official duties preserving peace and security."

That night, Tammy called me, crying her eyes out and nearly hyperventilating as she haphazardly related what had happened. I had recently returned from working for Dark Skies Security on a U.S. State

Department official's Personal Security Detail in Kabul, Afghanistan and was shocked at what my ex-wife was telling me. I had heard stories about this sort of thing while I was overseas doing my usual "Merc" work, but at the time I wasn't sure how accurate they really were. I told Tammy I would be right over. I made the drive from my apartment in Carlsbad on Laurel Tree Lane to her Loft in Gas Lamp Square on Market Street in record time. After I had drawn everything out of Tammy and Angela, I was filled with rage and anger unlike any I had felt in years, Sure, I liked killing people overseas for a living, but it was nothing personal, just business. This was one fucking hundred percent personal! Tammy and I had remained good friends even after our divorce and spending time with Angela was always something I loved doing after returning from my "contract" work in various foreign shit holes. Late at night in Tammy's apartment, I suppressed my anger while she cried on my shoulder, taking deep, calming breaths as Angela curled up in my arms and cried her eyes out, hugging me as tight as her thin arms would allow. I pressed her tightly into my chest and patted her head, telling her that everything would be alright and that Daddy would make everything better. For some reason, I had a quick flashback to the time I bought Angela a tea set to go with her doll collection and on the inside I felt like smiling when I remembered how happy it made me when she was happy. Then, the seething anger returned.

Yes, I would make things right, no matter what the cost, keeping all options on the table, but as I had first learned at Boot Camp from those rock-hard, humanoid gorillas known as Marine Corps Drill Instructors, the only way to properly take an objective was one step at a time.

First, I had to know more about what I was dealing with. So, I started "Googling" search terms to pull up all the news stories about abuses by the P.P.A. and sure enough, what happened to Tammy and Angela was not an isolated incident, although it was probably the worst one yet, at least that I know of. During my searches I read about all the robbery and sexually oriented abuses by the P.P.A. as well as the laws that had been enacted to protect their sorry, worthless asses. Let me tell you, it was quite a shock to someone like me, who could remember growing up in America when it was still America and not some more technologically superior version of an old East Germany. Of course, then again, what happened in years past with the T.S.A. at the airports should've served as a warning to anyone with half a brain (hey, even I can be a little oblivious sometimes). Our first course of action was to go to the San Diego Police Department ASAP since I read somewhere that the security tapes are only kept on file for 72 hours. Since the incident occurred downtown, we went to San Diego P.D.'s Central Division station at 2501 Imperial Avenue. We filled out all the necessary statements and reports before sitting down with Detectives from the Sex Crimes Unit. They were thorough in their questioning and also extremely courteous to all of us. Female officers were brought in to speak more with Tammy and Angela along with a representative from Child Protective Services.

Later, we all sat down with the two Sex Crimes Detectives, Bill Vargas and Shiela Ramirez. Detective Vargas and I hit it off right away as we had both served in the Marine Corps in the early to mid nineties. We were in the same Regiments, but different battalions. It turned out that both the San Diego Police and the Los Angeles Police Department had seen quite a few folks trying to file charges against P.P.A. screeners for a whole host of offenses. Since we weren't the first to come to San Diego P.D. with such a complaint, Detective Vargas told me that search warrants had already been put through for various incident files held in offices near the P.P.A. security checkpoints. The next day, Detectives Vargas and Ramirez executed a search warrant at Horton Plaza and recovered the security tapes from the secondary screening room. I was then able to see what had happened to my wife. All four of the P.P.A. employees were identified but when it came time to make the arrests, the reality of our Nation's most current laws hit me like a freight train in the night. Detective Vargas sadly admitted that the best we could hope for was to try to force the P.P.A. to fire the screeners since the courts had ruled that they could not be charged or even arrested if what they did was done while they performed their so-called duties! Because of this, the local court wouldn't even issue an arrest warrant as they not only felt that it would be futile, but that it would cause them to run afoul of the Feds at D.H.S. and perhaps cost the city of San Diego millions of dollars in Federal aid for emergency preparedness and so called First Responder training.

Detectives Vargas and Ramirez had only pursued our case in the hope that some sort of justice, no matter how small, could somehow be exacted on the perpetrators. Two of them, Joe Harl and the obese supervisor, Simon Cobb, were both convicted sex offenders while the dyke screener that initiated the incident, Lilith Caldera, had previously been arrested, though not convicted, for assault and battery and indecency with a child four years earlier. The fourth screener, Alberto Jimenez, had once been arrested for Grand Theft Auto in Los Angeles and we noticed from the security tapes that he had some sort of gang tattoo on his right hand.

All of this evidence just made things worse and to tell you the truth, I don't know who was more pissed off after that, me or the two Detectives. Detective Vargas seemed to be the more irate of the two. They both suggested that Tammy and I consider going to the media but after some discussion, we decided that it might be too much for Angela. I ended up just promising Tammy that I would find a way to take care of everything like I said I would. A few days later, Detective Vargas and I met at the Hooters in the

Gas Lamp quarter, had an enjoyable dinner being served by a tight-body waitress and then went outside to my black Ford Explorer in a parking lot across the street from the Borders bookstore. He told me about other cases of criminal abuse by the P.P.A. and before I could ask him why he had called me tonight and asked me to meet him here, he slid over a thick stack of files in a manila folder.

He just looked at me and said; "I'm sick and tired of watching criminals get away scott fuckin' free and I hate fucking pricks who are somehow put above the law just 'cause they work for the motherfuckin' Feds.[7] I know you're an ex-Jarhead, I know you're a fucking Merc, I know what you do for that shady goddamn firm Dark Skies and I know you'll do what needs to be done with what's in that file and don't let me ever see you back in my station after being arrested for anything!" With that, he clapped me on the shoulder and said "Semper Fi" before stepping out of the Ford and leaving.

Inside the folder was a plethora of information on all four of the P.P.A. shit birds who had molested my ex-wife and my daughter. This file had everything: addresses, mug shots, pictures, cell phone numbers, criminal records, billing information, what sort of cars they drove as well as their shift assignments and work schedules. "Fuckin A," I said to myself when I looked it all over. Pasted at the top of Lilith Caldera's files was a note telling me that in about three weeks NBC-7 in San Diego would be airing an investigative report on abuses by the P.P.A. and that the incident with Tammy and Angela would be mentioned since Detective Vargas had given one of the reporters clips of the security tape videos as well as copies of the police reports we'd filled out. It was time to get busy.

Having done my time in the Marine Corps before I became a Mercenary, I still had quite a few friends in various Law Enforcement Agencies who would be more than willing to help me out. The first was David Mendoza, a Border Patrol

Agent who did some digging and found out more about how the P.P.A. worked their shift schedules in and around San Diego. He also provided me with two accurate-as-hell Immigration and Customs Enforcement Agent badges for later use. According to what David told me, even employees of Homeland Security Departments knew not to ever get crossways with a Customs agent, what with all the power they had always wielded. Then, I contacted one of my old Merc buddies, Johnny Harris, a former Army Ranger who I first met when I went to work for the Executive Outcomes Mercenary Firm back in the late nineties. This was right about the time that it ran afoul of those banana republic, tin-pot faggots in the U.N. When I asked him to help me hunt every goddamn one of these P.P.A. cocksuckers down and kill them, he was more than happy to help. In fact, he was overjoyed at the prospect. A guy like Johnny Harris sure as shit would be. Hell, the crazy fucker used to love sticking cats in microwaves and interrogating insurgents in Sierra Leone by using a Black and Decker drill to bore through their kneecaps. I can still remember this one classic, Johnny Harris incident that occurred when we were working in Brazil as privately contracted military advisors to the Brazilian Security Forces. We'd caught this one whacked out narco-trafficker/anti-government terrorist and Johnny decided to have some fun with him. So, he strung the Brazilian insurgent up in a tree and then tried to coax this captured Anaconda the size of a drainage ditch into eating the poor fucker, legs first. Unfortunately, the Anaconda took too long for Johnny's taste. He ended up blowing the snake's head off with a 12-gauge Mossberg shotgun right about the time it had swallowed up to the guy's kneecap. Oh boy, was that a mess to remember.

On another occasion, when Johnny and I were at this bar in Cartagena, he went on about all that his ancestors had been through and said that one of them had even died during the Holocaust in Nazi concentration camp. When I responded with a "no shit," Johnny just said; "yeah the crazy fucker got drunk and fell off a guard tower!" That is just the sort of "whacked out" guy that Johnny Harris is and it just so happens that he hates dykes and women who try to be men just about as much as he hates rapists and sex predators.

This is why, right now, he was really loving it every time the dyke screener, Lilith Caldera, tried to wail in agony through the bloody, oil soaked gag tied into her mouth with tangled strands of duct tape.

Tracking Lilith Caldera hadn't been all that difficult with all the surveillance data Detective Vargas had provided me with. One night, after we tailed the nasty bitch back to her apartment at 1767 Oro Vista Road in Chula Vista, we just waited for her to go inside before I approached the door and knocked. When she answered, I flashed my I.C.E. badge and told her that my name was Special Agent Hardin of I.C.E. and that she needed to come with me to answer some questions, all of which pertained to a recent rash of security breaches around Horton Plaza that we thought were linked with a terrorist element trying to worm its way across the border. With only some minor haggling, she agreed to come along and I put my badge back into the dark trench coat I was wearing and we walked out to my Ford Explorer. After we got inside and drove off she finally started asking too many pointed questions in between pulls on her Marlboro cigarette. That was when Johnny Harris popped out of the rear floor and shot the bitch with a dart that had been filled with a highly potent tranquilizer called *sodium thiopental*. He said it would put her to sleep and fuck her up a little, but not kill her. Then, we drove across the border into Tijuana where Carlos Gutierrez, a Mexican cop I've known for years, led us to an abandoned warehouse that he said would be safe from any prying eyes. As was customary when keeping any corrupt Tijuana official in one's own pocket, I tipped Carlos three hundred dollars and he made sure we were left to our own devices and oh, how sweet it was!

After we flipped on our Coleman lantern, we bound and gagged Lilith

Caldera before tying her up and chaining her to an old rusty, but still solid, seventies era looking wheelchair that just wouldn't budge no matter how hard you pushed it. This would end up being better than one that would still roll and you'll soon see why. When Lilith awoke we took turns kicking the living shit out of her. After a while, I pulled back hard on her tiny crop of hair and yanked her head backwards so I could look her in the eye. I didn't care if she saw me or Johnny as it really wouldn't matter, considering what we had in store for the idiotic carpet-licker. Johnny moved in with a sledgehammer and proceeded to smash Lilith's toes one at a time on each foot. One by one they were crushed into tiny, pudding-like puddles of bruised flesh, bone and blood. As her body started to convulse in agony all I could do was smile as Johnny raised the sledgehammer in the air one last time and smirked like an adolescent viewing a Penthouse magazine for the first time.

Johnny let out a sharp grunt as he swung down towards the floor and a loud *SPLAATCH* noise interspersed with the echo of tiny bones being mashed into the pavement filled the warehouse. Lilith Caldera's entire body looked like it was trying to levitate itself into the air as muffled cries of agonizing suffering escaped through the rags stuck in her mouth. Then, her neck went limp and I thought she might somehow be dead until I checked for a pulse. Sure enough, the ugly cunt was still alive. I moved around to the other side of the chair and slapped her in the face until her eyes finally opened with the kind of horrified, shocked look a dog or a deer might have in its eyes after you've blasted half of their guts away with a shotgun.

I say, "That's right bitch, you better wake the fuck up and look at me!"

She takes deep, rapid breaths through her nose and keeps staring at me with confusion on her disgusting face. So, I decide to clear things up a bit. I pull a recent picture of my ex-wife and daughter and stick it in front of her eyes.

I grab her hair again and say; "You should remember these two, you know, the thin brunette with the pretty blonde daughter you and your nasty ass fuck stain friends stripped and molested at Horton Plaza a little while back! Come on BITCH, DON'T YOU FUCKING TELL ME YOU FORGOT HOW YOU TREATED HER AND MY DAUGHTER LIKE A COUPLE OF FUCKING GODDAMN COMMON CRIMINALS IN A SOME KINDA' WOMEN'S PRISON. HELL, I'LL BET YOU AND THE REST OF THOSE FUCKIN' PRICKS HAD LOTS OF FUN DOIN' THAT TO A COUPLE OF INNOCENT HELPLESS FEMALES WHO COULDN'T FIGHT BACK!!"

A sudden, focused look of recognition shows in her eyes as she looks at the picture again. Lilith's body visibly tenses up as her eyes seem to jut out of their sockets. Yep, the bitch remembers what she and her pals did and now, she damn sure knows she's going to pay dearly for it.

Through gritted teeth, in a low and cold tone I say; "Yeah, bitch, that's fuckin' right, the two pretty little things you decided to molest that day were my ex-wife and my daughter, my little girl, one of the few things in this world that I still love dearly. Now, you're gonna feel some serious motherfucking pain, sweetheart!"

I look over at Johnny Harris and just nod my head. He comes forward and drops a backpack on the filthy concrete floor and pulls out a plasma cutter and hooks its wire to the nearest electric outlet on a workbench near the main doors. He drops the cutter next to his backpack and picks up the sledgehammer. Another mischievous smile crosses his face as he takes a long swing and does his best to bury the heavy hammer into Lilith's left kneecap, causing jets of blood, tissue and bone to squirt out into her slacks amidst a resounding *CRAACK* that echoes loudly in the decaying warehouse. The gag in her mouth bulges out as she tries to scream in agony but she just doesn't quite belt out the normal notes with the duct tape holding everything in place.

Tears are bursting out of the P.P.A. bitch's eyes as she grunts and hyperventilates. Johnny repeats the process with the right kneecap and this time she shudders and spins about thirty degrees to the left. Her eyes seem to roll back in her head and I hold out my hand, signaling Johnny that it's time to finish what we started. After he grabs the plasma cutter we sit and wait for a few minutes before I slap Lilith again to wake her up. She looks like a hurt animal begging to be put out of its misery. That will come soon enough.

I look her in the eyes one last time and I say; "Well, I guess you thought you were real fuckin' tough and bad, humiliating a couple of helpless innocents, didn't you?"

She just stares at me with that deer in the headlights look and I lose my temper just a little.

I yell out; "GODDAMN YOU, YOU FUCKING DYKE ASS BITCH, YOU MOLESTED TAMMY AND MY LITTLE ANGELA 'CAUSE YOU'RE JUST A WANNA BE MAN TRAPPED IN THE BODY OF A WORTHLESS FEMALE PERVERT AND YOU'RE PROBABLY JUST JEALOUS THAT THEY'RE PRETTY AND YOU'RE SO FUCKIN' UGLY AND WORTHLESSAND YOU WISH YOU'D BEEN BORN A FUCKIN' MAN WITH A REAL DICK AND BALLS! AIN'T THAT RIGHT?"

She can't answer and right now all that comes out of her body besides blood and tears are animal-like cries that remain as muffled now as they were a few minutes ago.

I say; "Alright then, bitch, you're gonna pay, oh yeah are you gonna fuckin pay."

I step aside and Johnny fires up the plasma cutter and I have to help him hold Lilith's right arm in place as he completely cuts off her right hand, the tool's extreme heat cauterizing the wound and in the process making sure she doesn't bleed to death. This is especially good since I'm not ready to kill her, not just yet anyway. I stuff the severed hand in a Ziploc bag and seal it up. I had a little plan to use it in the near future.

We let her stay passed out for just a few minutes before kicking the crap out of her to wake her up, again. Johnny takes care to make sure Lilith sees the main part of the small explosives package we're sticking underneath the chair, putting it about a foot away from her ass and crotch. The explosives package has got roughly five pounds of C-4 attached to a cell phone triggered detonator/blasting cap combination inside it, but that's not all. There is a half a stick of dynamite "daisy chained" to the detonator with a string of Det-Cord (which burns/detonates at about 244,000 feet per second) hooked up to a second blasting cap. I made sure to duct tape the truncated stick of dynamite high up on her right leg where it met her thigh, putting it extremely close to her crotch. She squirmed and screamed and all I could say was "yeah bitch, how's it feel?" Not wanting to set the warehouse on fire and draw any unnecessary attention to our little rendezvous, I grab the Coleman lantern off the counter top and chuckle while thinking about how much fun this has been.

Johnny pulls a cellular phone out of his pocket and says; "Ok, Miss Lilith Caldera, wannabe rug-muncher queen of the Amazons, when me and my partner walk out of here, I'm gonna use this here cell phone to dial the number of the one that's tied in to the detonator on that bomb and that stick of dynamite taped up on your fuckin' thigh. When you hear it ring, you'll have about five seconds to contemplate what's gonna happen and then BOOOM!!" Both of us laugh with genuine joy and amusement at her current predicament.

We open up the main warehouse doors and before we make ready to leave, we look at each other and laugh again. Johnny starts to dial in the other cell's number and I look at Lilith Caldera, the dyke who molested Tammy and Angela, now tied up fifty ways to sundown in a decrepit old wheelchair, her knees and feet smashed beyond recognition or use.

All I can say is: "Now run for your life bitch!"

Johnny cracks up laughing as the other cell phone starts ringing and Lilith tries to scream to the world for help, as if it would do any fucking good. We leap outside and quickly close the door, taking cover behind an old 69' Camaro. Then, KAPOWWW!!

A split second later I hear the hard splattering sounds of wet clumps of partially incinerated, overpressure mutilated flesh, bone and muscle tissue slamming into the thin steel wall. It was time to look at our handy work. So, Johnny and I open up the sliding doors and peek inside with our Surefire flashlights and Holy Fucking Shit!

Lilith Caldera wasn't anywhere near being completely blown to pieces or even dead, but that's how we wanted it to be. Both of her legs were totally blasted into incinerated mulch below the knees and her right leg from the upper thigh on down had a gigantic, partially blackened, blood spewing, oblong chunk blasted out of it.

It looked like a Jurassic Park Velociraptor with white hot teeth had tried to eat the inner half.

There were also shredded, mutilated clumps of crushed bone and blackened meat where her ass and pelvic areas used to be while much of her upper body remained somewhat intact, even though it was still partially burnt and viciously contorted in a horrific pose of suffering as it was still strapped to the eviscerated wheelchair. A fetid flow of air-bubble-plastered blood gurgles its way out of her bruised mouth in between her lips and what was left of the rag we had stuffed in it. The red flow was followed by a sort of superficially muffled, high pitch wheezing noise succeeded by a partially choked scream that she just couldn't force all the way through her lungs and throat. Her eyes were still wide open, tears of desperation pouring out with fear and traumatic shock visible behind her blue irises, and all of it seemed to say "please finish killing me now!" Sorry woman, no such luck tonight. I stand there for just a while longer and stare until Lilith's upper body, the only part with much of anything still left, starts to jerk and twitch, her eyeballs finally rolling into the back of her head.

"Ya' think she's still alive, bro?" asks Johnny.

I say, "fuck her, who gives a shit. The cunt can keep on suffering for all I care!"

Johnny obviously sees eye to eye with my train of thought because he just slaps me on the shoulder and jogs out of the warehouse knowing I'll be right behind him. After hopping back into my Explorer we drive out of Tijuana and head north through San Diego on Interstate Five. I would drop Johnny off at his place in Oceanside before heading home. We'd be meeting up the day after tomorrow for another "gig" against those P.P.A. fuckers. When I get home tonight, I'd start sorting through both my modest assortment of cash bought, disposable cellular Trac-Phones as well as my little collection of fireworks. I could only hope that the cops in San Diego were still antsy and trigger happy after all the recent terror alerts and security scares. Hell, with all the scares and alerts following the wave of suicide bombings, San Diego patrol cops were now required to carry submachine guns and flak vests while on duty. According to one news report, some cops patrolling around downtown were packing the infamous Black Talon hollow points. They were especially paranoid after the news stations reported that recent intelligence reports indicated that Al-Qaida planned to target police stations. That should make things even more interesting.

Downtown San Diego. 1:58 pm. West Broadway and 3rd Avenue.

Sitting in the passenger side of Johnny's Toyota Four Runner, catty corner from the Horton Plaza Mall, provides a great observation point from which I can monitor the P.P.A. shift change set to take place in exactly two minutes. The forward most part of the mall used to be a normal front entrance to the Sam Goody music store. Crowds of teenage girls chatting away on their cell phones along with smiling, happy parents used to stroll around here enjoying the clean, pleasant ambience, mentally secure in the knowledge that they and their carefree children could be content with the time spent. Such pleasant scenes of enjoyment and freedom were now rotting on history's garbage dump.

The fountains and benches had been demolished to make way for an enclosed, roped off security line and a tiny P.P.A. employee parking lot, all of it surrounded by a ten foot high chain link fence topped with cyclone strands of razor wire complete with vicious looking warning signs advising patrons of search procedures and the penalties for carrying prohibited items like firearms or knives. In order to stay on good terms with the P.P.A. and kiss their ass as much as possible, the gutless managers of the Real Estate company that owned Horton Plaza, clearly trying to emulate the Airlines and Airports, had posted signs which bluntly stated: "All persons entering Horton Plaza automatically consent to a thorough search of their person and belongings."

An automated voice recording reminded shoppers that each person, upon entering, must be ready to produce Social Security cards, Driver's Licenses and REAL ID and that each patron may bring only one personal carrying bag or purse, etc. As shoppers were curtly herded through the security lines by P.P.A. screeners wearing their brand spanking new, military style red beret headgear, the automated voice thanked them for their "cooperation" and soothingly reminded them that "security is everyone's responsibility." The computerized voice's advisories sure as hell fit the situation. In order to get through the front entrance's security line, shoppers had to be herded through a narrow walkway that went right down the middle of the razor wire fence complex, flanked on either side by detachments of P.P.A. screeners searching for random, secondary screening subjects as they paced around like carnival sideshow despots in paramilitary regalia. To the trained eye it all looked exactly like what it really was: a makeshift, half-ass detention center complete with sanctioned abuse of innocent Americans by a flock of dumpy looking, unkempt schmucks, many of whom did what they did only because they would never possess the toughness, brains and fairly solid background needed to hack it in a *real* military unit like the Marine Corps and Army or a *real* Law Enforcement unit like a city police department SWAT Team or the F.B.I. So, the jackasses took P.P.A. jobs where they could get their jollies off with halfway decent hourly pay by harassing and robbing grandmothers, children and young females, none of whom would fit the profile of an actual terrorist. They all felt powerful and protected by the razor wire topped constructs that separated them from a more accurate form of reality and psychologically intimidated everyone else into submission. It was all a sign of the times.

I look at my watch. It's now 2:04 pm. Those two assholes Joe Harl and Alberto Jimenez should be coming out to their car any second now to go home as the two scumbags were actually roommates in an apartment in eastern San Diego. The employee parking lot was full this morning so the two jackasses had to park their old Chrysler Sebring. Go figure it, a convicted and paroled sex offending WASP living with a whacked out Mexican car thief.

I'm starting to zone out, thinking about what *they* did to Tammy when Johnny says, "Hey bro, here they come, get it goin'." I grab the black Trac-

Phone and dial 911 and after two rings the Emergency Dispatcher picks up and says, "nine one one, what's your emergency?"

I say, "Jesus Christ, ya' gotta listen to me, there are two fuckin' guys, I think they might be terrorists, they're in a beige Chrysler Sebring on Broadway Circle next to the Sam Goody store building by Horton Plaza. I…"

"Sir, calm down please. You say these two men are parked on Broadway Circle, now why do you think their terrorists?"

I say, "Look lady, I saw inside their car while I was shopping. They got Uzis, shotguns, machine guns, grenades, all kinds of funky shit and the guys who came in that car, I heard 'em talkin' in Farsi or some kinda' like foreign language or somethin'!"

The dispatcher tries to interrupt but I cut her off.

I yell out, "Look dammit, after they got through jabberin' in that shit they were talkin' in, they switched to English and I heard 'em say a lot of shit about the police station. I think they're comin' to blow up a police station. Goddammit, you gotta fuckin' get cops here now and stop 'em! I saw some big, heavy ass vests in the back of the car too!"

"Ok, sir, you saw multiple assault weapons and explosives materials inside a Chrysler Sebring parked on Broadway Circle between Sam Goody and the NBC building and the two guys that got out were talking about a police station. Correct?"

I say, "Yeah, that's right and get cops here quick 'cause they're about to drive off!"

She asks me, "Sir, can you read the license plate?"

I say; "Uh, yeah, it says GBT-X40." She repeats the plate number and I say, "Yeah, that's it now hurry up!"

"Try to stay calm sir, it'll be just a moment." Her voice clicks off for a few seconds and then comes back on.

"Alright sir, we've dispatched multiple units down there to Horton Plaza. Now who are you and where are you located at?"

I lie and say, "My name is Randy McCoy and I'm at the corner of Fourth Avenue and Broadway and, oh shit, they see me, I think they're gonna make a run for it!"

"Mr. McCoy the police are on their way, just stay calm," she says.

I click off the Trac-Phone and watch as Joe Harl and Alberto Jimenez each light up a cigarette and chew the fat as they strip off their black P.P.A. blouses. They're taking their time and are obviously not in a hurry. Harl, the chubbier of the two, starts up the car and looks for a break in traffic. He starts to cruise out of his parking spot when suddenly, like a bat out of hell, four black and white San Diego Police cruisers, sirens blaring and lights flashing, come barreling in and screeching to a grinding halt, all up and down Broadway Circle only a few feet away. Joe Harl slams on his brakes and looks around in confusion, sensing that something bad was going on.

If only the jackass could've known.

After the last cruiser had squealed into place and cut off any possible escape, the police officers leaped out and drew down on Harl and Jimenez with everything from three Sig Sauer pistols (most likely .40 caliber) to five H&K MP-10 submachine guns. All of them are screaming at the top of their lungs for the two scumbags to get out and put their hands in the air.

The tallest cop, the one with Sergeant's stripes and another nice big Sig Sauer, seems to scream the loudest.

He keeps screaming; "GET THE FUCK OUTTA' THE CAR, RIGHT FUCKIN' NOW GODDAMMIT, GET THE FUCK OUT OF THE CAR, KEEP YOUR HANDS WHERE WE CAN SEE 'EM MOTHERFUCKERS-GODDAMMIT RIGHT FUCKING NOW!"

Another cop gets on his squad car's loudspeaker and repeats the instructions for them to get out right now and put their hands in the air. By now, I've gotten out of the truck and lit up my own cigarette by a garbage can, putting my right hand in my blue jeans pocket and waiting.

The rest of the cops, four males and two females, start yelling louder for the two P.P.A. punks to comply or else get shot to hell. They start to move in a little closer but stop, obviously wary of what might happen if any bombs in the car were to go off. Well in front of the cops, panicking mall shoppers scurrying around under the Sam Goody and Citibank logos are being rapidly herded away to some sort of safety by screaming P.P.A. personnel when Jimenez and Harl finally put their hands up with the latter screaming; "Hey man, what the fuck? You motherfuckers can't do this shit, we're goddamn Federal Agents, man!"

The cop with the big Sig Sauer closest to Broadway Street, visibly agitated, yells out; "GOD FUCKING DAMMIT, I AIN'T TELLIN' YOU AGAIN ASSHOLE, GET THE FUCK OUT, LAY DOWN ON THE MOTHERFUCKIN' GROUND AND PUT YOUR FUKING HANDS BEHIND YOUR BACK! RIGHT THE FUCK NOW!"

Then, he grips his lapel communicator and yells something into it before settling back in to his Weaver stance. Harl and Jimenez start to open their doors as they make ready step out of the car. I notice that Jimenez drops his hands away from the windshield as one of the cops moves up behind the car, still keeping his MP-10 submachine gun straight and level. It's now or never. I take the two M-80 firecrackers out of my pocket and I light them with my Bic and toss them in the garbage can as I turn back towards the Four Runner.

A split second later I look back toward Horton Plaza and suddenly the firecrackers go "CRAACK POWW." I thought that from a little distance they'd sound just like two gunshots going off and the cops obviously agreed. The tall cop with the Sig Sauer shot first, putting five well placed rounds right through Joe Harl's neck and chest, sending crimson gouts of blood and bone scraps flying inside the Sebring right before his companions cut loose with a lethal barrage of hot, hollow point lead. The cracks of pistol shots and the short, static, "BRRRRP" sounds of three to five round bursts of submachine gun fire tore through the windy daytime air as nearby pedestrians screamed in terror and fled from the scene in a panic. Since he was the one actually facing the cops, Joe Harl caught the brunt of the dozens of high-velocity rounds that were fired. All the car's windows were either cracked or shattered as Harl's disgustingly fat body was either shredded by flying debris or punctured over and over again from all directions by rounds from the spooked police.

Behind Harl, Alberto Jimenez's head, face and neck were blasted apart and partially torn to shreds by what were obviously multiple bursts of .40 caliber Black Talons fired from by the cop who had moved up on the car's rear before I detonated the M-80s. The pudgy Rent-A-Cop who had been guarding the gate to the small P.P.A. parking lot nearby was cowering in fear on the pavement and it looked like some of Alberto's clumpy brain matter along with some ricochets had impacted his crummy white guard shack. More chunks of glass and metal were blasted into the air before the cop with the Sergeant's stripes finally yelled; "CEASE FIRE, CEASE FIRE, GODDAMMIT CEASE FUCKIN' FIRE!"

The gunshots stop and an eerie silence seems to fall over the area. Harl and Jimenez were shot to fucking hell and the driver's side of their car was turned into a nasty looking metal ventilation duct on wheels. The whole shooting had lasted only a few seconds but to those cops it probably seemed like hours. I hop back in the Four Runner and Johnny slowly cruises out on Broadway and turns right, heading west. It won't be long before the police start sealing off this whole area. I'll bet those NBC News employees looking down at the shooting were about to shit themselves in excitement. When the shooting gets investigated, the cops won't end up being in that much trouble. Last night, Johnny and I had followed Harl and Jimenez back to their rat chewed apartment and we planted some evidence in the car. Basically, Johnny and I just taped two blocks of C-4 into the undercarriage along with a metal box containing two fully automatic MAC-10 Uzi variants with Black Talon ammunition stored in two separate magazines. When the police conduct a thorough search of the car, they will quickly find these highly illegal weapons as well as the plastic explosives. At the bottom of the metal box containing the two MAC-10s is an internet street map printout of the San Diego Police Department's Central Division station, with the red star marking its exact placement repeatedly circled in dark red pen. The name that I used on the 911 call, that of Randy McCoy, was not fictitious. It just so happened that the P.P.A. Regional Security Director for all of Southern California was named Randy McCoy. Maybe that would stir up something strange and unpleasant for the sorry bastard. Scumbag shit birds with criminal records aren't the only motherfuckers who can play dirty.

After we pass the Santa Fe train station going north on Kettner Boulevard, I think about stickdeath.com, the website which originally gave me the idea for the firecrackers in the trash can. Damn that shit was so fucking cool. Then, I think about the next P.P.A. shit bag we're going to kill and I look over at Johnny Harris and flash him a shit eating grin. He just smirks and looks back towards the freeway entrance, knowing that what I had just thought of would be pretty fucking nasty, vicious and cool as hell.

Two days later. 11:36 pm. 3498 E Street. Vlad's.

Parked just down the street from San Diego's hottest Swinger's club, Johnny Harris and I are starting to get just a little overcome with excitement at the prospects of what we were going to do to Simon Cobb, the P.P.A.

Supervisor who had, for lack of a better word, "supervised" the molestation of Tammy and Angela. Oh yeah, this fucker was going to feel pain and suffering the likes of which few could imagine. Johnny Harris and I are like two little kids chomping at the bit to go into a candy store when Simon Cobb emerges from Vlad's, his hair a mess and his shirt un-tucked as he walks to his car, a silver Chevy Volt Hybrid. I think to myself that it only figures that a damn pervert like Cobb would frequent a place like this and then Johnny says; "Holy fuckin' shit, man, I'm never goin' to this shack again, not with that asshole's spooge germs all over some couch or a goddamn floor."

Well, Johnny always did like variety in his life when it came to women, even if it did involve a perversion of sorts. I say nothing in response and quietly snicker instead.

As Simon Cobb slowly drives west on E Street, I whip my Explorer around to follow him. Once we get behind him, Johnny leans forward from the bench seat behind me, turns on the small, square red and blue flashing lights we stuck on the dashboard to make it look like we were plainclothes Detectives on official business. Simon had surely been subjected to quite a bit of questioning lately by San Diego P.D. so our appearance shouldn't surprise him too much. It wasn't long before he pulled over and stopped, obviously waiting for us to come to him. I exit the car and walk up to the driver's side where Cobb had already rolled down the window. I flash my counterfeit I.C.E. badge and say; "Mr. Cobb, I need you to step out of your car and come to my vehicle to answer some questions."

"But officer, ah, sir, I've already been questioned by you guys a helluva lot for all this shit, what's the deal?"

I say, "Mr. Cobb, my partner and I are Immigration and Customs Enforcement agents and our questions do have a lot to do with what happened at the security gate with the two females, but don't worry, it's nothing bad. In fact, we think one of them might have been a MULE running heroin for a Mexican Drug Cartel. If you can step over to my vehicle and confirm a few things that were seen on the security tapes, it would help us out a whole lot. We'd be pretty pleased and maybe we could talk to your bosses and get you promoted. How does that sound?" I show him my I.C.E. badge again, this time putting it directly in front of his face.

Cobb shrugs his shoulders and says; "Ok, if ya' put it that way, yeah, sure, I'd be more than happy to answer any questions you guys got."

He steps out of the car and walks on my left towards the Explorer and I gently steer him to the passenger side door behind the driving compartment, the red and blue flashing of the halogen lights casting an eerie, surreal, pulsating glow around us.

I open the back door and say, "Now, my partner is gonna show you some photos so you can confirm a few things for us, alright?"

He just nods his head, a hooded look of mild apprehension starting to appear in his eyes right as I bury the heel of my right foot into the bundle of nerves behind his knee, causing him to collapse to the ground, his knees bouncing off the metal outcropping below the open door with a light *thunk* and a scrape. Before he has a chance to get out much of a cry for help I push a black cotton pillowcase over his head and down to his neck before pulling back on the fabric's slack and jumping forward with all of my weight and slamming his head into the floor and spinning him around with Johnny trying vainly to pull me off. With rage boiling in my veins, I sock him as hard as I can, right square in the solar plexus, knocking the wind out him. Then, I jam my right knee into Cobb's crotch over and over again and I feel his neck flush red as I try to pound his balls and rib cage into fine white powder. Johnny grabs the fucker by the mandibular pressure point located up and under the jawbone, easily yanking him inside the vehicle and literally slamming the barrel of my Colt .45 pistol to his head after cocking the hammer, splitting the forehead skin wide open and drawing blood.

"Don't you fucking move or try to fight asshole," says Johnny through tightly gritted teeth as Cobb bucks and twitches in agony.

For good measure he hisses; "Cause if ya' do, I'm gonna fuckin' blow your fucking little prick off and then I'm gonna rip open your stomach and make motherfuckin' balloon animals with your intestines."

Johnny looks at me and I nod in return, my heart pounding with the receding of the adrenaline surge as I get back in the Explorer and drive off, even more anxious than before to get to our next destination, way outside the city limits.

2:53 am. One mile North of Pound Road. El Centro, California.

The musty, mold spore infused smells of the old, long abandoned farm house were finally disappearing as the nostril searing odor of gallons worth of high octane fuel took over. We had soaked nearly every square inch of the house's interior with gasoline taking great care to leave the immediate areas close to the dilapidated kitchen counter as dry as possible. After all, we didn't want Simon to burst into flames before he had a chance to suffer. Simon Cobb moaned and cowered under the Coleman lantern's sharp glow, his cries muffled by duct tape and his adipose-infused legs partially useless after we smashed the living hell out of them with a sledgehammer. Well, the duct tape might've been overkill since Johnny cut out a huge chunk of Cobb's tongue, but what the hell, if you're going to fuck up some no good shit bag, then why not go the extra mile. Once we were satisfied that the house would go up like a Texas A&M bonfire when lit, Johnny and I each slipped into a tear-away Tyvek suit and put on gardening gloves and surgical masks. I cut open the crotch to Simon's slacks with my razor sharp bayonet, grabbed his ball sack and sliced off his nuts in one fast motion, blood spewing out all over the front of my suit. As Cobb convulsed in pain and nearly jerked both himself and the rusty chair he was tied into up in the air, Johnny moved in with a portable, propane powered blow torch and buried the searing, bright blue dart of flame right into the spurting, bloody maw left by my bayonet, completely cauterizing the gaping wound in well under a minute.

Cobb's head rolled back and forth like it was possessed, just before he passed out completely. I check for a pulse and his heart beats are only slightly irregular, but still strong. Fuck it, we'd wake this fucker from his beauty sleep shortly and then set him up for the grand finale of viciousness, or justice, depending on how one looks at it. Me, I thought it was poetic justice to the twenty-eighth power and Johnny, well, he was simply my friend and he liked killing people, especially if he or someone he knew thought that the victim just flat out deserved it. Oh well, the two minutes have gone by.

We take turns slapping and kicking Cobb until he wakes up and looks at us, a cry for mercy emanating from his bloodshot eyes. Johnny and I wouldn't even try to show this prick one iota of mercy. Besides, when it came to giving mercy, guys like us just sucked at it anyway, so why bother.

I stuff Simon's tongue lump and testicles into a plastic Ziploc bag and seal it shut. It was time to show this cocksucker the meaning of perverse enjoyment. We untie Simon, dragging him over close to the mildew stained kitchen sink and standing him up in front of the wooden counter top. I cut away what's left of his slacks and underwear and he struggles only a little bit against the obscenely tight metal handcuffs that restrain his hands behind his back. Johnny pushes Simon up against the counter and I whisper in his ear.

I say, "Simon, do you remember the pretty brunette and the young blond that you strip searched and vaginally assaulted a while back? Well, do you, you miserable fuckin' shitbird?"

In the ambient glow of the lantern I see the affirmative answer in his eyes. More beads of sweat are bursting out of his pores as his body begins to shiver in terror. I tell Simon that it was my ex-wife and teenage daughter that he and his cronies hand raped and then I let him know how much I still love my ex-wife and how deeply I adore my daughter. They are, after all, one of the few things of beauty I have left in this life of aggression and killing that I chose for myself so long ago. However, a prick like Simon doesn't really deserve to know all those little details, now does he?

As a sendoff to hell, or wherever else it is that scumbags like Simon go when they die, I say, "You know, I'll bet you just wanna tell me how you're not really a bad man or even a perverted, spineless sack of shit, you were just doing your job, albeit a little overzealously right? Well, motherfucker I'm doing my job as the ex-husband of that woman and the father of that girl. You see, hombre, I was born and raised in Southeast Texas and back there, this is how husbands, fathers and brothers deal with worthless, humanoid monsters like you!"

With that said, Johnny stretches Cobb's dick out all the way to the old light socket on the wall by the sink and I raise my hands up in the air, taking in a deep breath. My hands come down hard and I drive the thin bayonet all the way through the hilt of Cobb's prick and into the wooden counter top.

The asshole tries to scream in agony, but nobody can really listen or care, except maybe Lucifer's minions who I imagine we've been spoiling a little of late. Johnny grabs the sledgehammer and starts hammering the bayonet handle while I hold it steady. Soon, we drive it almost all the way into the hard wood of the kitchen counter, leaving the tip of the handle not too far from the bottom of Cobb's pelvis. With his hands cuffed behind his back, the piece of shit couldn't remove the knife no matter how bad he wanted to. If he passed out and fell down or couldn't stand up for hours or days on end until he was found, his dick would be slowly sheared in two right down the middle. As far as I was concerned, Simon's options were just a little too easy. For good measure, Johnny dribbles some gasoline on the counter where Simon's dick nearly meets the wall. Oh, man is that going to sting. He looks over at me, his eyes still begging for mercy as if he wanted us to just kill him and get it over with. Oh fucking well, that was just too damn bad.

I say, "Simon, in a second, we're gonna walk outside and light this whole motherfuckin' house on fire with a Molotov cocktail. Yeah, that's right, this whole place is goin' up in flames after we leave! So, you've got two choices! One, you can try to run away and claw your way out of a burning, boarded up house with crushed kneecaps and broken shin bones, thereby getting only partially incinerated. Of course, you'll have to slice your cock in two in order to do so and man, that's gonna fucking suck having an immolated body and no male sex organs left. Two, you can save yourself the pain of mutilating the only physical traces of manhood you've got left and either become a crispy critter or pray someone finds you. You figure it out there, buddy."

We walk outside and bolt the door back into place right before going out to the Explorer and grabbing the Molotov cocktail, in this case a bottle of Jack Daniels with a thin sheet of cloth stuffed down the top. Johnny hands it to me and with great pleasure I light it and hurl it through an exposed window above the dining room. First, the whole room catches fire and then, *WHOOOSH KRUMMPF*!

We back away and shield our eyes from the scorching blast of heat as the whole freaking house bursts into flames like a canister of JP-4 jet fuel lit off with a firecracker. I watch as the fire starts to engulf the kitchen like a descendant of Prometheus vomiting fireballs and then, I see a burst of flame shoot up in front of the old window above the sink. It looks like the gasoline by the tip of Cobb's excuse for manhood just lit off. We jump back into the

Explorer and make ready to haul ass away from the scene. Before we peeled out, I could've sworn I heard a sickly, hoarse, sub-human reverberation coming from the kitchen. Sayonara Simon!

10:28 pm. Five nights later. 1307 Laurel Tree Lane, Carlsbad.

Leaning back in my La-Z-Boy chair, I down the last gulp of beer in the Corona bottle. I was watching the rest of the latest three-part NBC 7 Investigates program on abuses by the P.P.A. A number of women were interviewed with their faces blacked out for protection and the incident with Tammy and Angela was discussed in fairly surprising detail. No mention was made of the recent disappearance of the screeners involved. When asked how he felt about the abuses, Regional Security Director Randy McCoy stated yet again, that:

"We in the P.P.A. want everyone to know that we take every complaint of abuse very seriously and that we are very *concerned* about the issue. But people must understand that if one of our employees becomes too uh, aggressive, that we are living in scary times that require these sorts of security policies. Still, we are going to strive to improve our Customer Service procedures for shoppers everywhere."

What a lying sack of bureaucratic shit this guy was. He and his family would, of of course, be exempt from any of the search procedures once he flashed his REAL ID card followed by his P.P.A. Clearance Disk. Reminding this idiotic fuck-head that it was a shit load of fucking ragheads that snuck across a still open border who blew things all to hell would obviously have been a waste of time.

The last person to be quoted for the third time in as many weeks was the P.P.A.'s local area Spokes-broad/paid shill, Kelly Walters. All she could say was; "Being a woman I understand everyone's apprehension over our policies, but I want everyone to know that we are all very *concerned* about these abuses."

There it was again, the word "concerned," the favorite key word of overpaid government Spin Doctors. Yeah, I'll bet her dumb ass was really fucking concerned. This was all such a fucking load of bullshit and a fair number of Americans still bought into it. Although, judging by what I heard at some of the more awesome, popular eating places like Mary's off North Coast Highway in Oceanside, a lot of folks were finally starting to wake the hell up and realize that they'd been had.

Oh well, no matter.

At my request, Jack Sprigg, an old Marine buddy of mine who had recently retired from a career as a communications surveillance specialist for the National Security Agency, and now worked as an aggressive but effective Private Eye, had dug up a ton of useful info on Randy McCoy and Kelly Walters. Right now I had everything from their cell phone numbers to their email addresses and the license plate numbers of their cars. I was about to have some serious fun tormenting this asshole, but first I had a special package to mail to his nice, cozy condo inside the Peckham Lofts complex in downtown.

I slip on another Tyvek suit with thick welder's gloves and a surgical mask before going to my refrigerator and removing Lilith Caldera's severed hand along with Simon Cobb's testicles. Keeping the hand and balls in their Ziploc bags, I stuff them inside another, larger, vacuum sealed bag and into a previously prepared package filled with a shit load of Styrofoam peanuts and then put it all in place. Of course, I'm going to address it to Mr. Randy McCoy at 1045 Sixth Avenue, San Diego, CA, 92101. In order to have it mailed so as not to be traced back to me I would employ two effective countermeasures, one of which was both really fucking cool and nasty as well.

First, I would have another close friend of mine who works as a UPS driver, take the package well into San Diego before dropping it off at the downtown Post Office from where it would actually be postmarked and then promptly delivered to McCoy's nearby address. This way, no one would see me walking around with it or delivering it in the city proper or anyplace remotely close to where I live. Second, the return address would be listed as: Kelly Walters, 1307 Laurel Tree Lane, Apartment 205, Carlsbad, CA: 92009. Yes, that's right, the holder of the return address would be the local area Spokeswoman for the P.P.A. who didn't seem to think that what happened to Tammy, Angela and others was that big a deal. You see, Kelly Walters lived just on the other side of the Apartment complex I reside in. In fact, I had recently "chatted her up" and gotten her to go out on a date with me just last night. We had dinner at a first class restaurant in the Gas Lamp district called Johnny Love's. After eating a great steak dinner and consuming a decent amount of alcohol, she opened up and told me about how one of her bosses, Randy McCoy, who just happened to be married, had sexually harassed her and demanded sexual favors in exchange for a quick promotion to Regional Spokeswoman. At first she bristled at his advances, but eventually, she gave in and let him fuck her a couple of times after hours right on his office desk.

Kelly ended up not getting the promotion because some other P.P.A. gal named Geena Morris fucked him more often and gave great blowjobs. I sat and listened to her whine and gripe and in return got to hear her moan like a fifty-dollar whore later on that night. All things considered, she was a pretty good fuck and later, while she was asleep, I leaned over with my switchblade knife, cut a hole up under the mattress and stuffed a dime bag of heroin up inside it. This put the drug not just inside but way in between the mattress and the bed frame where she would definitely not find it even after changing the sheets. This stunt's outcome could be saved for later. Right now, I was writing out a note to be stuffed in the package next to the sealed body parts which, in my best forgery of a female's flowing handwriting, read: "*Hey jerk, after all the times I fucked you and let you put it in my ass, you still fucked me over and didn't promote me. Here are some body parts me and my brother decided to send so you'll know what happens when you fuck with me!*"

Yeah, it seems a bit of a stretch to do this to frame a woman, but Kelly Walter's brother, Tommy, was a paroled convict who was not only convicted years ago of possession of a controlled substance (heroin), robbery and assault with intent to commit murder, but was reportedly known by both his family and the Carlsbad Police to harbor feelings of lust towards his sister, some of which became apparent when he had tried to kill one of her old boyfriends in high school. Besides, it directed the cops away from me and back at the ranks of the P.P.A., whose head butting battles with local Law Enforcement were already being documented by the San Diego Union Tribune. Not to mention the fact that Randy McCoy's wife, Barbara, would likely see and read the note right before or right after they saw the body parts.

I place the note on top of the styrofoam packing and tape the package shut. I'll give it to my UPS pal tomorrow morning along with a fat cash tip of one hundred dollars for the extra trouble. I'd finish off Kelly Walter's life soon afterwards.

Twenty-two hours later. 8:28 pm. Plaza Camino Real. Carlsbad Mall.

Parked outside of Sears next to the Transit Center, I lean back in the driver's seat of my Ford Explorer and click on the second Trac-Phone I bought yesterday. I slowly dial the number to the Carlsbad Police Department's Vice Unit and when the female desk Sergeant answers, I say, with a slight Mexican accent; "Yes, I'd like to let you know that one of my neighbors, Kelly Walters, is dealing lots of drugs, like fucking crack and shit to kids out of her apartment."

The sergeant says, "Sir, who are you and how do you know this?"

I say, "I'm afraid to give my name, man. I mean, she's got this crazy brother named Tommy who'll fuckin' kill my ass if he finds out I told you. Look man, I was in her apartment and I saw her stuffing dime bags of heroin under her mattress and shit. You guys like, need to go arrest her or something and get her crazy ass brother too!"

"Sir, can you tell me where this woman lives?"

I say, "Yeah, I sure can."

I proceed to give the lady cop Kelly Walter's full address, occupation and the exact location of the dime bag of heroin inside her mattress. I also make sure to let the cop know that on a few occasions I've seen Kelly Walters transport dime bags full of heroin for her "tweeker" brother by stuffing them way up inside her pussy where they could remain fully concealed.

Then, I hang up and drive off towards Vista Way where I'll stop somewhere, wipe down the Trac-Phone and throw it away. Such an anonymous tip will be investigated by the police as it does establish what the law classifies as either "good faith" or "probable cause." Her brother's nasty criminal record should help with the latter and who knows how San Diego P.D. would pursue the severed body parts mailed to Randy McCoy since they would have to work directly with Carlsbad P.D. in the process. Well, the destruction of Kelly Walter's life was set into motion as was the terrorizing of Randy McCoy and his wife. Now, what dirty little things could I do to fuck up this smarmy, asinine bureaucrat's soon to be unhappy life?

Suddenly, ideas start popping into my brain housing group and I decided that my last few days inside the United States would end up being fairly enjoyable.

11:53 am. Internet Café. North Coast Highway and Mission Avenue.

Waiting for the computer to boot up, I lean back in my leather chair and smirk as I think about what I saw going on at my apartment complex this morning. On the way to my Explorer what to my wondering eyes did appear, but Kelly Walters being led away in handcuffs as Detectives from San Diego P.D. and patrol cops from Carlsbad executed both search and arrest warrants before ransacking her apartment. There was no doubt in my mind that they would soon find the "stash" inside the bottom of her mattress. As for what might happen to her at a police station, well, that interesting chunk of information on where she liked to hide the drugs should have some bearing on what kind of body search she would have to undergo. As a P.P.A. employee she should certainly understand the necessity of having her twat canal yanked open. The thought of it makes me chuckle like a teenage meth-head watching a cat burst apart inside a microwave. Oh fucking well, don't support dishing it out if you can't take it.

After the computer powers up I click on the Internet Explorer Icon and start perusing a few of the adult oriented sex service websites for the San Diego/North County area. As soon as I find the ones that allow someone to place personal sex service ads, I skip to the homosexual sections and start typing in some of Randal McCoy's information. The online ads only require contact information to go with the written sale slogans, not pictures, which makes it all fairly easy. The slogan I type into the first one, hothomostuds.com is the same as the others I'll use and it just states:

Hot Gay lover needs other horny men with lots of muscles and tons of nasty lust and don't be afraid to bring whips and chains! See you soon, Big Boys! Please send nude pictures if you want an appointment! Ask for Randy.

Then, I type in Randy McCoy's home phone number as well as his office numbers which are (858)-456-7895 and (619)-234-5654, respectively. For email information, I first list the one that both he and his wife use, (randyandbarbara@abl.com) and then put in his work email: mccoyr@ppa.gov. For good measure I repeat this whole process twice before doing it one last time in the Personals Section of the San Diego Press, the city's premiere underground newspaper, all the while paying online with McCoy's actual VISA Credit Card number obtained by my old pal, Jack Sprigg. Placing his home contact information would go a long way to fucking up his personal life and marriage while the printing of his work number and email would surely get him in deep fucking shit with the powers that be at the P.P.A., who closely monitored all of their employees' incoming and outgoing emails.

Now, I could proceed to jack with Randy McCoy's oldest son, Roy (a college student at U.C.S.D.) and make life even more unbearable for both he and his wife. Since this fucker thought it was just fine and dandy to either just order or simply permit his uniformed automatons to physically and sexually humiliate *my* daughter, then I saw no reason why I shouldn't return the favor in spades on one of his offspring. With Roy McCoy next on my shit list, I close out the web pages, pull up Microsoft Word and start typing out a bomb threat note that reads:

> *HEY YOU MOTHERFUCKIN' BLACK AND WHITE PIGS, I'M SICK AND DAMN TIRED OF GETTING' SPEEDING TICKETS FROM YOU JACKASSES EVERY TIME I LEAVE CAMPUS! YOU ASSHOLES NEED TO LEAVE ME THE FUCK ALONE OR ELSE I'M GONNA DRIVE BY WITH A*

BUNCH OF PLASTIC EXPLOSIVE BOMBS AND BLOW YOUR IDIOTIC ASSES INTO SMITHEREENS! WHY DON'T YOU ALL GO FIGHT REAL CRIME OR GET A REAL FUCKING JOB!

Once it's finished, I print it out, delete the file and stuff it back in my backpack with the information files from Sprigg and walk over to the front desk and pay $7.75 for the roughly hour and a half I spent online and go into the one person restroom, making sure to lock it after I go inside. I sit down on the toilet and slip on two layers of latex gloves before delicately wiping down the threat letter with a wet wipe and carefully folding it up and placing it inside a pre-addressed envelope. I wet the seal with a small damp sponge instead of my tongue.

The return address was Roy McCoy's P.O. Box at the University but the sending address was to a Detective Wilkinson at the San Diego Police Department's Central Division. With that done, I walk down the street to Mary's Family Restaurant, one of the best places to eat breakfast in Southern California. The smiling, courteous and pretty blond waitress grabs a menu and escorts me to a booth in the back and asks me what I want to drink and I just say; "coffee please." Sure thing, she says and goes to get it. I look at my watch and see that it'll still be a while before Johnny Harris arrives to meet me. So, when the waitress returns I order the Waffle Combo and sip my coffee, savoring ever last drop until my food arrives. I devour the awesome entrée of eggs, bacon and a Belgian waffle and when I'm about done, Johnny Harris shows up and slides into the booth in front of me.

Darting my eyes around and seeing that no one's looking, I pass a plastic bag containing the threat letter envelope to Johnny underneath the table. He slowly grabs it and I say, "Make sure that gets to our UPS pal when we're through."

He nods and places it in his jacket, his face, like mine, is all business now.

Tomorrow night, the two of us would be leaving everything in the U.S. behind except the bulk of the money we'd earned from our various merc contracts overseas, most of which was already in offshore accounts that we could easily get to once we were south of the border. To guarantee us safe passage through Tijuana, Johnny had struck a nice little deal with Octavio Alvarenga, one of the local drug cartel leaders. We would help train paramilitary troop contingents to protect some of his cocaine shipments coming from Mexico proper and Central America. In exchange, Johnny and I would be able to work in Tijuana temporarily before heading off to various Central American locations to teach the drug cartels' private armies how to counter all of the "gringo" tactics and technology. While working these new jobs we'd have to also work our stock in trade around places like Cozumel and Aruba. Getting through the border crossing with the few weapons we'd be carrying with us wouldn't be an issue since some of Alvarenga's minions already had two night shift Border Patrol agents and a Customs Officer on their payroll. If I wanted to make my original employer from many years ago, the American government, pay for what they did to my ex-wife, daughter and so many thousands of others, this new gig was a damn good way to do it.

"Everything's five by five and good to go down south," answers Johnny as if reading my mind. "Outstanding," I shoot back. Nothing more needed to be said. I trusted Johnny as much as he trusted me and if he said that everything was good to go, then it was so.

I say, "See ya' tomorrow night bro. You know where."

Johnny just nods and gets up to leave. I wait a few minutes before leaving a generous, well deserved tip for the attentive, bubbly, polite waitress and paying the bill up front. While collecting my change, a news alert on CNN catches my attention. It appears that the Islamic Coalition of America was suing not just the P.P.A. but the real estate company that owned a shopping mall in Phoenix for what they alleged was "racial and religious profiling of a despicable nature." Apparently, two towel-heads talking animatedly in Arabic were forced aside and made to take off their shoes after being wanded. According to what I was seeing on CNN, the P.P.A. was making numerous public apologies while stating their willingness to settle out of court even after they terminated the employment of the screeners involved for what they agreed was "horrible misconduct." I had to take a deep breath to keep my heart rate under control after hearing this load of insane bullshit. Every fucking day, innocent, ordinary Americans, women, children and the elderly were routinely groped, harassed, molested, robbed and treated like prison inmates at airports and malls by both the T.S.A. and the P.P.A. for the god awful crimes of buying airline tickets or going to shop for gifts. Yet, as long as the victims were Caucasian, Asian, African-American or Hispanic, the P.P.A. stood by its employees and blew it all off like it was no big deal, knowing they'd never be held accountable by either pro-government Democrats or "compassionate conservative", i.e. Socialist Republicans. If my ex-wife or daughter get manhandled and abused then that's Ok. However, if some fucking Arab foreigner or some shady Middle Easterner who fit the profile of all the other towel-heads that killed so many thousands of Americans got so much as looked at wrong, then all of a sudden there was a need to investigate the incident, terminate employment and pay reparations.

Oh fucking well, fuck it all. I'd be out of this mess soon enough and what the hell, maybe I'd get another chance to fuck with the P.P.A. on the way out. For some reason, that's exactly what my gut instinct was telling me.

11:48 pm. South on the I-5 Freeway near Chula Vista.

We're getting closer to the Tijuana border crossing and it feels sort of like a great burden is about to be lifted off my shoulders as I start to push the

Explorer past 70 mph. I never thought I'd feel that way about leaving my own Nation on my way to a place much more chaotic, but for a man with my skills and past deeds living in such Orwellian times, I guess that's what it had finally come to.

My train of thought is rudely broken when Johnny slaps me on the shoulder and points to an old 2007 Hyundai Elantra cruising south along side of us. At first, I wonder why the hell Johnny is pointing at the young driver and passengers in the car and then, in the glow of the interior light switched on by the driver, I see that two of them are wearing bright blue P.P.A. uniforms complete with red berets tucked inside their military style epaulets.

"Holy fuckin' shit. There's at least two of 'em right next to us," quips Johnny.

"Hell, let me grab somethin' and waste the fuckers. We're almost to Mexico, the

cops ain't gonna catch us in time if we do it real freakin' fast."

"Hold on," I say as I steal a second look at the driver. "Two of those fuckers look Mexican. Shit, lets just keep goin' and see if they go across the border too." Johnny looks tense and disappointed until we see that they're going to Tijuana just like us. Now we could kill the bastards deader than a Rwandan Drag Queen at a south Alabama Klan rally and get away with it.

After being pulled aside by the agents and the Customs Officers on Alvarenga's payroll to be "searched" and found to be "clean," we cruise into Mexico, quickly catching up with the Hyundai Elantra a couple of miles south of the border and passing it not too far from our agreed upon rendezvous point with Alvarenga's men at the Arts and Crafts Market off Avenida Negrete and Calle Segunda. I slam on the brakes and the Elantra skids to a stop behind us before tapping my rear bumper. The driver's probably wondering what the hell's going on. The asshole would find out soon enough.

Johnny and I reach back into the Explorer and yank out two Benelli M4 semi-automatic 12-gauge shotguns loaded with .00 buckshot before jumping out of the Explorer and running back to the Elantra. We click on the Surefire flashlights hooked under our barrels and a painfully focused beam of light illuminates the car, temporarily blinding the P.P.A. occupants as we move in. Flicking off the safety I scoot up to the driver's side, staring down the weapon's Picatinny Rail sight and as he lowers the window and starts to hurl curt questions and curses at me, I jam the barrel against his nose, crushing cartilage and pulling the trigger. BOOOM!

The driver's entire face and part of his mouth burst apart in about a dozen directions as the middle of his entire cranium shoots up in the air and seems to levitate away from the chunky crimson miasma of exploding anatomy that now covers the entire front part of the car's interior, washing the other two passengers in a spray of flying lead and exploding gore. The other front occupant, a female, screams in terror as the rear passenger, another young male, frantically tries to escape out the back only to have his neck and face eviscerated by a combined explosion of buckshot and glass shards after Johnny fires a round straight through the right rear window. Not wanting to waste anymore time, I aim my Benelli's barrel at the female passenger's leg and fire.

BOOOM!

The stock bucks into my shoulder and I have to close my eyes after my face gets pasted again with blood and bone.

Her left knee and thigh explode outward and are jerked towards the floorboards by the inertia of the blast. Johnny breaks open the passenger side window with his shotgun's stock and pulls the woman out by her hair, briefly snagging her red beret on broken glass before kicking her in the back of the knees and slamming her to the ground. I jump across the car's hood, not wanting to miss this little finale.

Johnny lets go of her hair and literally tries to bury the barrel in her cheek, probably knocking out teeth in the process. He fires and the woman's entire face, nose and jaw line are blasted towards the ground in a bursting crush of powder burnt, pink mouth tissue and crushed stew of flowing blood and shattered teeth. There was a gigantic mutilated hole where her nose, mouth and chin used to be. She certainly wanted to scream but couldn't since she no longer had a tongue to speak of. Ha, now there was a pun I could savor.

We root around in the car and ransack the driver's wallet to make it look as much as possible like another gunpoint Tijuana tourist robbery gone awry. After hopping back in the Explorer and finishing the short trek to our rendezvous point, the realization that I may not ever be able to return to my own Country finally hits me. Yet, as I reflect, I realize that it still could've been a hell of a lot worse. I could've been caught and arrested or even killed. Thank God Jack Sprigg and Detective Vargas were kind enough to provide me with all the information I needed to get revenge and exact *my* version of justice. I could rest easy knowing that Tammy and Angela would be well taken care of. Over the years, as I worked numerous Mercenary jobs overseas and did Private Military Contract work in Afghanistan for Dark Skies Security I had amassed quite a fortune, much of which I had given to Tammy in various allotments. This way, I could make sure that she was financially secure and that Angela's college could be paid for.

During these last few days I had transferred more money to her account by writing her "gift" checks for a thousand dollars here and twenty-five hundred dollars there, never going up to five thousand since anything of that amount or more had to be reported to the Securities and Exchange Commission. As time goes on, I'll still be sending her some fairly generous money deposits here and there, even though by now I've made her perfectly secure as far as money goes. I would make sure that the estranged wife I still love and the little girl I cherish so much are well taken care of. For now, they would be alright, but who knows how long they or anyone else would remain safe from the tentacles of an increasingly parasitic government. I would soon have to go about setting up an "out" for them so that if need be, they could be brought overseas to Cozumel, Aruba or the Caymans. For the time being, my old buddy Jack Sprigg would look in on them from time to time and if necessary, bend over backwards to help them in any way he could.

Yes, I would still be making a ton of money doing all the destructive things that I've gotten so good at and yet, I felt depressed and sad when I thought back to my childhood. It was a better era, a more *American* decade, when I grew up hunting, shooting and fishing in Tomball, Texas, at a time when we could still keep shotguns and rifles in our cars when going to high school as "latch-key" kids of the Eighties, back when we had an awesome President who did all he could to get the government out of our personal lives while he put the fucking commies in their place and Freedom was just as cool as Hockey-Masked Jason or Freddy Krueger.

I look back north towards the border and the American in me makes me want to shout, "Where in God's name has my country gone?" I think everyone back in America knows the answer to that question, but it'll become one they don't want to answer for fear of actually having to look in the mirror.

THE END...for now.

A TALE OF TWO HOUSTON ROBBERIES

June, 2000. 11:38 pm. Northwest Houston, Texas. Timewise Texaco station on Grant Road and North Eldridge Parkway.

"GET THE GODDAMN FUCKIN' MONEY BITCH, GODDAMN MOTHERFUCKIN' SHIT ASSHOLE! HURRY THE FUCK UP, GET ALL THE MOTHERFUCKIN' CASH RIGHT FUCKIN' NOW OR I'LL FUCKIN' SHOOT YA' I'LL BLOW YOU'RE FUCKIN BRAINS OUT ALL OVER THE GODDAMN FLOOR, YOU FUCKIN' PUNK ASS BITCH! HURRY UP!" screamed the shorter of the two strung out, pale white, inbred Jed junkie "tweakers" turned robbers. He gestured gangster style and repeatedly pointed and swung his snub-nosed .38 caliber "Saturday Night Special" revolver at 19 year old convenient store clerk Andy Stanford. The junkie robber's last swing scraped the pistol's barrel across Andy's scalp, drawing blood. The teenage clerk, already scared stiff jerked backwards, threw his hands higher in the air and pleaded;

"Ok, Ok, Ok, I'll get the fuckin' money man, alright, alright?"

Sweating profusely, Andy opened up the register and tried to grab the money, his hands shaking uncontrollably, but was violently shoved back by the taller robber, the one with the knit cap and a wooden baseball bat he had already used to smash the register and the soda fountain. After ransacking the register, the bat swinger turned to his pal with the gun and said; "This ain't all it man, there're tons more in the safe, I know dat' shit "cause I used to work at one a deez' places. This gaw'damn skinny ass punk can get it!"

"Shit, fucking hell, why won't these assholes take the damn cash and go. I knew this would happen as soon as Mr. Laubach left and shit, when was my Uncle Ray gonna get here, he'd be armed," thought Andy.

The gun man snarled, spat and shoved the barrel back into Andy's face, screaming even louder; "WELL GO ON BITCH, GET IT ALL OUTTA THA' FUCKIN' SAFE, I AIN'T GOT ALL NIGHT!"

"Look Man, I ain't got the combo to the safe, I'm not allowed to have it I swear," answered Andy.

"BULL FUCKIN' SHIT MOTHERFUCKER, GET IT ALL OR I'LL BLOW YA' FUCKIN BRAINS OUT AND ASS FUCK YOUR CORPSE, YOU FUCKIN' LITTLE PUNK ASS BITCH..."

For a split second, Andy looked down towards the middle shelf under the counter and above the black safe. Holy shit! In the middle of the fiasco, he had forgotten about the two weapons his manager, Jim Laubach, had hidden and set up under the counter. Jim Laubach was no ordinary seventy-six-year-old day manager. He was a retired U.S. Marine Gunnery Sergeant and a veteran of the hard winter battles of the Chosin Reservoir during the Korean War and as such, he believed in staying armed at all times.

Taped to the underside of the counter-top in a nylon holster was a Smith and Wesson .44 Magnum, loaded with six Remington Gold Sabre hollow points. But that wasn't what Andy decided to grab first: He was about to go for the double barrel twelve gauge shotgun that was mounted and locked in place on two Y-shaped stands on top of the shelf above the safe. It was set up so that in addition to remaining hidden from the view of any nosy customers, it was mounted with its twin barrels facing right up against the counter's wood paneling, meaning that it was pointed at either the knee or crotch level of anyone who got close to the counter-like the asshole with the gun. From where he stood, it looked to Andy like the barrels were pointed right at his kneecaps. Andy knew that Jim had loaded the shotgun right before he left to go to the Wendy's on Louetta Road. In fact, this shotgun of Jim Laubach's was originally made for duck hunting and had been sawn off to its current length. The two shells loaded inside were 12 gauge three and a half inch magnum rounds, nearly twice the size of a normal 12 gauge round, with each one packing loads of .00 buckshot.

The two hammers had already been cocked back and two strings had been tied to the triggers so Andy or another clerk could reach down inconspicuously and pull the triggers that way. Were it not for the gun being waved in his face, Andy would have to fight to keep from smiling. It was now or never.

"Alright, alright dude, I'll get it for ya, I'll get it like right now."

"WELL HURRY UP FUCK FACE..."

Andy took a deep breath and quickly dropped to his knees, making like he was punching in the safe's electronic combination. He grabbed the strings and jerked back with all his might, nearly ripping the shotgun out of its supports and setting off two high powered loads of high velocity buckshot blasting through the wood counter and tearing right through the gun swinger's kneecaps and quadriceps. The twin blasts roared through the store, tearing apart the shorter robber's legs while propelling wood shards into the other's thighs and crotch, puncturing and shredding flesh and muscle.

At first, the pistol waver's face went blank in shock and then, as Andy looked up, his entire upper body seemed to drop to the floor below the counter with a short string of wet, macabre, crunching and ripping sounds. The taller robber had dropped his bat after falling on the end cap of the snack aisle. He screamed and cursed as he gazed upon what had happened to his accomplice.

"Oh Fuck, oh goddamn, oh fuckin' shit man, motherfuck..."

An inhuman scream of agony welled up from behind the register as six futile, un aimed gunshots rang out below the counter as the short robber realized that he was much shorter than before.

Andy jerked the .44 Magnum out of its holster and cocked before looking up over the red counter top. The extremely close range of the double blast of the two shot gun shells had almost completely disintegrated both of the "tweaker's" knees and totally ripped both of his legs in half. His two legs, from the top of the shin bones down were swept aside, spread akimbo below the register. The rest of them, from the lower thighs on up, were a bloody, mutilated mess attached to a writhing, crying, wailing, blood soaked, half-man junkie who had just pissed his pants and was screaming as if on his way to hell. He would be shortly.

"OH GODDAMMIT, OH FUCKINNNNGG, HELLL, OHHH GOD YOU MOTHERFUCKKKERRR, OH FUCKING GOD MY FUCKINIINNGG LEGS YOU ASSHOLE," *sniffle, sniffle*, "OHH GOODD, AHHHH, I'LL FUUUUCCKINNG'' KILLLL YOU OHHH FUUUUCK!" His face turned a dark crimson from all the screaming he did.

Andy breathed in the sickly sweet scent of cordite mixed with blood and viscera. He was still shaking as he made eye contact with the taller thug. Andy watched him get up, gritting his teeth in pain as his eyes glanced at the high powered revolver. With his hands still shaking from a vast surge in adrenaline,

Andy gripped the .44 in both hands and brought it up, shooting the shotgun amputee prick right in the mouth, although he was aiming for the chest. A bursting red hole appeared where the junkie's lips had been as a splattering glob of teeth, bone, blood and nerve tissue erupted on the ceramic tiles underneath his head. The enraged look in Andy's eyes must've said, "you're about to die asshole," because barely a second later, the surviving crook tried to make a run for it.

His wrists starting to spasm from adrenaline, Andy fired two quick shots.

POWW. POWW.

He was shaking so much that his aim was way off and both rounds missed the thug's head and instead slammed into two bottles of cheap wine, spewing glass and amber liquid on the floor.

Andy ran in front of the counter, chasing the limping crook outside towards the stone walls of the Lakewood Forest subdivision, trying to line up the pistol's sights on his back. He heard police sirens off in the distance. Although his mind barely registered the sounds, it didn't matter since real help was a lot closer.

A quarter of a mile further down Grant Road, fifty-three-year old Ray Brock, an Army Veteran, ex-Cop and professional Rodeo Bulldogger turned Master Farrier, leaned back in his brand new Ford Ranger truck and slowed down as he passed the Diamond Shamrock Station. He was already ten minutes late to meet his nephew, Andy, but he didn't want to get a ticket for speeding-he had enough of those. Besides, Andy wouldn't mind. Funny thing though, he could've sworn that he heard gunshots a few seconds ago. Maybe he was imagining things.

"Fuck it, he'll love my new bumper stickers," thought Ray.

On the tailgate was a painting of an M-14 assault rifle above the words "In 1969 This Is The Only Woodstock I Remember." On the bumpers were two other stickers. One had a Skull and Crossbones set above the phrase "Kill'em All Let God Sort'em Out." The other just stated; "**Guns** don't kill people, **I** kill people."

The second he got within sight of the gas station's lights, Ray knew something was wrong. Some skinny kid that looked like Andy was running outside with a gun chasing after some limping guy in a big jacket.

"Oh, fuck," he said.

Andy must be running down some damn robber.

Oh shit, the robber was running towards the road.

Andy leveled the sights on the robber's back and fired.

POWW!

He missed the upper back where he was aiming and clipped him under the right shoulder, the heavy hollow point boring through muscle and bone as it mushroomed. The thug stumbled and jerked around to face Andy and it took his brain a few seconds to register what happened next.

Ray heard the pistol's report, saw the runner spasm and twist around, hunched over in pain, near the middle of the road and quickly put two and two together. He floored the accelerator and rammed into the crouched thief at roughly thirty-five miles per hour, cracking ribs and dislocating the wounded shoulder. The robber was knocked forward and slammed to the ground right before Ray ran over his chest area with both tires. After the "*THWWUNK*" of the impact, all Ray was felt was a mushy, Texas speed bump.

He slammed on his brakes and put the truck in park to see if his nephew was alright.

Andy sprinted up to Ray and lowered the pistol after as he looked through the ambient light of the gas pumps at the half-crushed body of the robber, whose mouth was still spewing blood and curses. The dying thug flipped Andy the middle finger and then did the same in the direction of Ray's stout and imposing frame. The latter action was a serious mistake.

"Well you simple minded son of a bitch," cursed Ray as he walked over to his truck and pulled out his Mossberg 12 gauge. After jacking in a round, he fired two loads of Number three buckshot at the thief's head and face, turning them into flesh covered "slushies" of gore and knocking chunks of concrete off the road.

The police sirens were getting closer but neither Ray nor Andy were worried for unlike many States, Texas was dead serious about allowing people to use firearms to defend themselves in any way from all sorts of thugs and miscreants.

All the arriving Harris County Sherriff's Deputies would say after investigating and watching the store's security tapes was: "Well, that's two less shit heads we gotta screw with."

The shooting of the thieving human shit bag brought back fond memories for Ray from his days as a soldier and a Cop. He decided it was time to call his old "youngster" friend Scott Raines and get back into the Mercenary business.

June, 2006. Thursday, 3:55 pm. 4950 Birdwood Drive. Southwest Houston.

Seated inside the driver's seat of a black Ford van with tinted windows, Arty "Skidmark" Burns, now one of Houston's Most Wanted criminals, massaged his wounded shoulder and unlocked his seatbelt. He glanced back at his four partners in crime. Tony Thomas, Ronny Jenkins, Mickey Shale and Martin Boggs were all zipping up their black jumpsuits and putting on ski-masks. They pocketed their knives and snub-nose revolvers with two of them picking up a makeshift battering ram and the others a couple of baseball bats, already stained with blood and brain matter. The four thugs and Skidmark Burns, their notorious wheelman, had formed their own little gang of brutal, home invading robbers one night over beer at a local honky-tonk after they had spent some time snorting crack and dealing Meth together. After their last two home robberies, the TV News Channels along with the Houston Police had named them the "kick door burglars" due to their infamous burglary techniques. These involved driving up to houses in west and southwest Houston in the middle of the day and smashing open the door to ransack anything of monetary value, which they'd then sell for cash to feed their drug habits.

One of the three robberies they had perpetrated last week not only netted them a ton of jewelry and DVD's, but some time to run a fast "train" on a big titted, thirty something blonde woman and her teenage daughter who happened to be home alone that day. They had just been getting out of bed when Skidmark and his crew rolled in and shut them up, pilfering what they liked and raping both of them. The daughter was the first piece of pussy Skidmark ever got without paying for it. She was tight as a vice too. Hearing her cry just made it better. Once they had what they needed, Shale executed both of them.

In another instance, it was just smash and grab with no one home but that last one was a fuckup. Some guy was home with a shotgun and scared them off with some volleys of birdshot. Skidmark's shoulder still ached where some of the tiny pellets had been crudely removed by Ronny Jenkins.

This robbery would be different.

They would use the battering ram to smash their way in, pillage the place and get the fuck out before the Cops could show up. There were no cars parked nearby and the garage door was shut. Skidmark told his fellow thugs that nobody was home and he felt confident making that assumption since Martin Boggs agreed. After all, Boggs was smarter than all of them since he actually made it past the tenth grade. The vicious robbers exchanged glances as they prepared to make their move on the small, one story house. Out they went, scurrying like sewer rats chasing urban refuse.

None of them could have known that lurking inside that house were three of the most lethal, professional killers in the city.

Seated around two couches in the living room by the front door, veteran Mercenaries Alberto Zamora, Friedrich Van Dokken and Joe Compton were in the final stages of reassembling their assault rifles and semi-automatic shotguns after having broke them down for cleaning nearly two hours ago.

The house belonged to Zamora, a retired Army Delta Force shooter who had recently left the service and taken a job for Dark Skies Security in Afghanistan supervising one of their Personal Security Details for high ranking Western diplomats after the Taliban had been ousted.

Friedrich Van Dokken had cut his teeth as a young soldier in the South African Defense Forces during the counter-insurgency wars with the Cuban backed Algerians and the ANC terrorists. In the mid nineties he had gone to work for Executive Outcomes, the infamous South African Mercenary corporation and had been hired by Dark Skies Security in 2002.

Joe Compton had gone to work for Dark Skies Security after eight years in the Marine Corps, the last four in the First Recon Battalion, including a tour in Afghanistan following 9-11 where he cut his teeth tracking down and killing multitudes of Osama Bin Laden's Taliban henchmen. After shooting some Muslim shit bags in one particular raid, he made the surviving prisoners dig shallow graves so their fellow terrorists' corpses could be buried with pig carcasses. Compton would take pictures of the dead bodies posed with pigs and mail them back to his Dad, who had served in the Marines during Vietnam.

All three of the men had worked together at one time in Afghanistan and Iraq and had become good friends as they all lived in Houston. Zamora asked them over for beers and they all brought their automatic weapons to clean them while "shooting the shit." As always, they'd each brought plenty of rounds and a couple of magazines for each weapon, just in case.

Zamora was racking back the charging handle on his M-4 Carbine, a spare magazine with twenty rounds of 5.56mm Extreme Shock Nytrillium composite, body cavity producing rounds by his La-Z-Boy chair. This type of ammunition nearly made Black Talons look like child's toys. Zamora had shot an Afghan in the leg with one of these composite rounds and it had blown an unbelievably huge chunk out of it, the wound cavity looking as if someone had used a red hot meat clever to scoop out his bones.

Freidrich Van Dokken was wiping down his AK-47 while Joe Compton sprayed WD-40 on his Benelli M4 12 Gauge shotgun, a box of shells in .00 buckshot by his side.

At that same moment in time, the four "kick door" robbers, thoughts of easy money dancing in their drug soaked brains, anxiously huddled up near the front door, which looked to them like any other door on any other house they'd seen.

It damn sure wasn't.

The three military contractors were talking about upcoming jobs in Iraq when suddenly Zamora got really quiet, the hairs on the back of his neck standing up as they had on countless missions when a sixth sense told him something was wrong. He shot a look over at the door, glancing at its plethora of extra locks and the wooden two by four braced against it as Van Dokken and Compton went silent.

The second Zamora slapped the magazine into his M4, the two other veterans followed suit and then, WHAAMMM, WHAAMM!

Someone was trying to break through the door. The three men sprang to their feet and began turning over chairs and couches to duck behind as they dropped into firing positions and locked their sights on the door.

"Wait 'til I say Fire," Zamora ordered.

The other two just nodded and waited.

Outside, Mickey Shale, Tony Thomas, Ronny Jenkins and Martin Boggs leaned back for a third time with the battering ram and put their backs into the next hit on the door. WHAAMM, CRUNNCH!

The door started to splinter. They moved back and hit it a fourth time. WHAMM, CRUUNCH! It was breaking open and Shale thought he saw a wooden board braced across the middle of the door. Fuck it! On the fifth try they ran back away from the doorway and got a running start, leaping back to the doorway and ramming it again.

WHAMMM, CRUNNCH!

The board braced against the door shattered while the middle of the door gave way. Jenkins and Boggs used their bats to smash away the rest of the door and kick their way in. When Boggs dropped the battering ram and stepped through the doorway near the living room, he froze and was shoved aside by Ronny Jenkins, who barely got the words, "Hey Boggs what the fu…" out of his mouth, before the living room erupted in a withering barrage of gunfire.

Three of the four robbers heard the roar of the Mercs' weapons right before they felt the pain of having their bodies shot to hell and blown apart. Boggs' head took two three round bursts from Zamora's Carbine, the Extreme Shock rounds turning it into an erupting miasma of brain and bone that made a nice Rorschach blot on the wall.

Jenkins' chest, neck and head were simultaneously punctured and bored by blasts from Compton's Benelli and Van Dokken's AK, the hollow points of the Soviet made .30 caliber rounds and the buckshot tearing up his vital organs and making Sushi out of his face. Tony Thomas turned to run away but was nearly cut in two by the rapid fire convergence of two streams of automatic weapons fire and a .50 caliber rifled slug loaded by Compton after he had used his last buckshot round on Jenkins. The three killers then blew apart Thomas' head while Mickey Shale, the only one still standing outside when the firing began, screamed and yelled; "Holy fucking goddamn shit fuuuck, fuuck me FUUCK!"

Three stray AK-47 rounds tore into his right hip and shoulder while wooden splinters tore into his skin and popped into his eyes. He screamed and wailed. Then, he turned to run.

Skidmark Burns saw what was happening and had no intention of hanging around to help Shale. He was just about to throw the van in gear and get the fuck out of dodge when he looked right towards Shale and saw his whole body halt in a spasmodic stop while his head literally exploded, a blast of gore soaking the front of the van and spewing out on the street.

"Oh God, oh God, oh fucking hell, oh shit, oh shit, oh motherfucking shit, I don' wanna die," he yelled as he threw the van in gear.

Standing on the lawn where they had chased Shale, Joe Compton stood up, lowered his Benelli and inserted one more buckshot shell and two more slug rounds in the breach. That last .50 caliber rifled slug he fired did a nice job on Shale. The other two Mercs reloaded and all three opened up on the van right as Skidmark *tried t*o speed away.

As he was about to floor the accelerator, Skidmark almost thought he'd make it when loud popping noises and shattering glass preceded by the report of rapid fire weapons brought him back to reality. His right shoulder exploded in hot pain right before his right hand was blown apart by a 7.62 AK round. Short, accurate automatic bursts blew through his now nonexistent passenger's side window and ripped up his right arm and rib cage. Suddenly, the crook of his left arm was blasted into bloody scraps of sinew and then he finally hit the accelerator, lurching forward as the trio of professional soldiers chased after him. He heard more gunfire and then his lower jaw was turned into a fleshy, high velocity stew of teeth and exploding tissue by a three round burst of Zamora's Extreme Shock rounds.

He jerked the steering wheel too hard to the left and the van swerved and flipped over on its side. He would've screamed but his tongue was in pieces scattered over the steering wheel and his T-Shirt. All he could do was make a wheezing sound and spew out more blood and shorn tissue. More bullets bored through the floorboard, flying into the steering column and punching through his feet.

The three professionals converged on the front of the van and turned Arty "Skidmark" Burns into the ugliest Corpse of the Month at the City Morgue.

Barely thirty seconds later, a fire team of Houston Police cruisers came screeching to a halt on Birdwood Drive. The Officers drew down on the gun toting Mercs with a mix of pistols and shotguns. They dropped their weapons at the Officers' instructions and waited for the questioning that would undoubtedly come.

Following close behind the arrival of the police cruisers, was a white Ford Crown Victoria driven by a tough as nails Navy S.E.A.L. Veteran of S.E.A.L. Team Six. The man in the passenger side seat, who he was currently charged with protecting, was Brian Cochrane, a veteran C.I.A. Case Officer who had come to Houston to set up an "off the books operation." They'd heard the gunshots and simply followed the police to the location of the shooting. Sure enough, there was Zamora, another well known "Private Military Contractor" for the Agency and one of Cochrane's favorite killers, surrounded by anxious cops. Cochrane knew Zamora would owe him big time if he made *this* crap go away.

Bill Carpenter, Cochrane's old C.I.A. Clandestine Services mentor from the Cold War days would be pleased with his latest progress report on their plan to blackmail Mercenaries into killing terrorists in the near future. Carpenter however, would have to remain superficially involved from a distance as he now resided in Switzerland. After select members of Congress had gotten wind of his past back alley dealings with the Russian Mafia, Carpenter had been left with no choice but to get the hell out of Houston and leave his firm, Mercury Securities, to some underling named Aaron Reynolds.

Cochrane had been asked by Carpenter to come into Houston with a scheme of maneuver to continue to insure Houston's protection and to wipe out what he knew were residual terrorist elements still residing in the city. Carpenter figured they had been hunkering down for a while to avoid the wrath of the Russian Organized Crime resulting from the quid pro quo deals he negotiated with them. Additionally, the writing was on the wall when it came to future tensions with Iran and the old C.I.A. Veteran knew that at some point in time, they might make a move against Houston, as it was one of the Nation's most vital economic centers.

Cochrane was moving into the city to set up and help orchestrate that protective "scheme of maneuver." He smirked while watching the Mercs get "proned out" by the Police.

After assuming the position on the pavement, Zamora started to think about the fastest way to get out of this mess. He had high connections in the U.S. State Department and the C.I.A. that he figured they could use to get out of trouble once the cops found the grenades and the M203 launcher he kept in the house. Well, this was Texas and *they* had just killed five disgusting, cowardly thugs that H.P.D. had been looking for. Zamora felt certain that Brian Cochrane could take care of this at his end from Langley once he called.

If only they had known.

THE END...for now.

HOLLYWOOD CENTERFIRE

A Scott Raines Story

November 9th, 2006. 7:52 pm. 702 World Way, LAX. Los Angeles, California.

Two nasty, no good shit bags were going to die by my hand tonight and as always, I would enjoy every fucking minute of it. Thoughts of brutalizing more assholes who deserved to die coursed through the corridors of my brain housing group as I crossed World Way to the nearest concrete median opposite the huge parking garage complex and stood under an aerodynamic gray tube that hung from the ceiling. The tube sported a bright green sign that announced in white block letters: LAX FLYAWAY BUSES. This is the bus line operated by Los Angeles World Airways that runs back and forth every thirty minutes between all the LAX Terminals and Los Angeles Union Station downtown. I unzip my black leather jacket in preparation for riding the heated bus. The cold, flesh-chilling night air does absolutely nothing to sober up the warm thoughts I have of ending more lives and raking in a chunk of dough for it.

At 9:00 pm, a height challenging Fly Away bus the size of Zeus's first toy truck pulls up and I hop up the stairs to sit towards the back, where I can see and observe everyone else who piles in. They all look like your average jet-lagged, hassle weary travelers either going to visit family or struggling to make a buck to feed themselves and give to that bloated, abusive parasite we call a central government. The last person in is a middle-aged Mom dragging three small children behind her. I'm the kind of guy who takes pride in butchering the assholes who prey on folks like these. The bus lurches as the driver merges into the cyclic flow of airport traffic and soon we are cruising down the freeway on our way to Union Station. As we plough through heavy traffic on the 110 freeway, I look around out my right side window and take it all in, knowing, as a seasoned killer and covert traveler, what lurks beneath it all.

Beneath a piss yellow veneer of streetlight barriers, the infamous South Central District of Los Angeles is a heavily patrolled, gunshot racked, urban blockade that woke up on the wrong side of a concrete smashing, pre-Apocalyptic torture session.

At night, Los Angeles itself is a gargantuan, vapor haze shrouded, electrically infused, multi-colored, sodium illuminated patch of semi-cybernetic, asphalt gutted urban noire cityscape on critical but failing life support.

Through the bus windows on the left side, I see the starkly lit fantasy façade of a stuttering metropolitan heartbeat visible above a freeway torn, geographically contained, concrete cordoned layer of pain, suffering and cold blooded murder; all of it superficially segregated by modern real estate realities and a herd mentality from obscene wealth, lust and decadence. To the east and the south, rival splatterings of humanity behave like too many rats in a cage while butchering one another like animals and shooting each other's brains out with weapons smuggled in from their mother country. To the far north and northwest, horny, lustful, financially cunning, cash bloated elites waste money on funding government sponsored protection rackets for baby whales and shit eating dirt rats to assuage their guilt for being born with gold marijuana pipes in their mouths. At night, they snort cocaine through silver straws sporting gold trim. If you are some poor bastard in the middle, the lower end parasites stand ready to rob, rape and kill you while the upper crust royalty emits wine soaked epithets of disgust when you fight back as the local government remains on standby to confiscate your legally purchased implements of self-defense, long after its had time to tax you into an earlier grave. If you're a motivated, tough street cop, don't try to stop a crime in progress or protect the saps in the middle or you'll be investigated and prosecuted. Los Angeles is what the rest of America will look like in twenty years.

This city is unique in that it was made into a household name by Hollywood even before it was turned into something darker and more infamous by its twisted gang wars and high profile murders of sickening depravity. If it were to die tomorrow, the city's Funeral Hymn would be a brain wave disrupting cacophony of wailing police sirens, crashing Low-riders, "slangin" gun fire reports, organ busting echoes from hypersonic boomboxes and a roaring howl of patrol-car-punctured human aggression as ethnic riots swallow up every welfare office and opposing architectural achievement from the past sixty years. After applause from the Kodak Theater, the final verse would be played out when whatever is left of the coerced, leach weary middle class, kills for protection and blows up City Hall before marching to Bellaire and Brentwood with pitch forks and torches to break out the guillotines. The gum chewing, "bubble headed" blondes from the Valleys would try to yammer away on their cell phones as they were turned into human fuck cushions. The flames engulfing the city would carry a mixed odor of cocaine, botox and silicone.

The man giving the city's eulogy would be a stereotypical "Limousine Liberal" aided by a Rolls Royce Rambo with an offshore account. The pallbearers would represent the ignorant son of a bitch who has killed every Republic and liberal democracy with the power of universal suffrage: John Q. Public.

None of the dumb shits flanking the casket or watching the procession would be aware of the fact that the grave diggers were obscenely wealthy, Big Business corporate types while the gardeners laughing their asses off and celebrating would be illegals and other assorted immigrant groups. The grave marker would be a giant, gold Oscar and the epitaph would be written in a dozen foreign languages, the first of which would be Spanish. The death of Los Angeles would be a harbinger of America's future urban fate.

I shake it all out of my head and focus on the job at hand.

Ahead of us, the downtown nightscape is an ochre soup covered, spear cluster of brightly lit, cloud ripping office buildings sitting high above everything from high end restaurants to blocks of tin shielded stop-and-robs and streetwalker stomping grounds.

After the bus parks behind Union Station, I walk to the ticket booth and pay the required $3.50 for the ride *from* LAX and walk through a platform at the rear of the transit center. The interior is cool and mildly noisy as I trot down marble steps and stroll through Union Station's main concourse, looking straight ahead to avoid making eye contact with the LA County Sherriff's Deputies who are passing me on their way outside. Instead, I glance to my right and pretend to take note of the electronic signs displaying departure times for the AMTRAK and Metrolink trains, just as any normal traveler in blue jeans and a leather jacket would usually do. Hanging a left,

I take the escalator down to the Subway's Metro Red Line branch. I go to the ticket machine, put in $1.25 and go down another escalator to the Red Line. Even though my two targets are in Hollywood, I decide to skip the Red Line branch that goes all the way up to North Hollywood and instead, hop on the one that shuttles back and forth between Union Station and Wilshire and Western. I needed to run some counter-surveillance routes to make sure I wasn't being tailed.

As the secondary Red Line shuttles back and forth, I periodically get off at random stops and wait to see of the same person or persons keep getting off with me. Once I'm sure my trail is clean, I get back on and ride back to the Seventh Street Metro Center where I hop on the Red Line that goes to North Hollywood. On the way, I run over the details of this "hit" in my head.

My two targets were an in-bread, methhead drug addict named Billy Ray Cobb and his slutty girlfriend/third cousin, Bobby Wilson. Not too long ago, Billy Ray Cobb and his brother Jimmy, had beaten and sexually assaulted a pretty young black girl named Lucinda Rockwell who worked as an exotic dancer at an Atlanta, Georgia strip club. She was in the middle of giving Billy Ray and his brother private lap dances and as the two brothers got even more drunk, they tried to force Lucinda to give them blowjobs, which she refused to do. Their response was to slap her around, cover her mouth and rip off her thing to molest her. Billy Ray's family girlfriend, had cheered them on with cultured phrases like, "C'mon Billy, make that nigger bitch squeal!"

Luckily, another dancer heard the commotion and after walking into the curtain shrouded booth, screamed and ran away to call 911. Atlanta P.D. arrived and arrested all three of these scumbags after they interviewed Lucinda and the other dancer who saw the assault. However, it was not an open and shut case. Jimmy Cobb was kept in custody since, according to the dancer eyewitness, he was the one whose fingers were doing the actual vaginal molesting. Billy Ray and Bobby Wilson, both of whom had served time for distributing Methamphetamines, were to be charged with accessory to sexual assault and were each released soon afterwards on eighty thousand dollars bail. To make a long story short, a meth dealer friend bailed them out and then they skipped town and journeyed all the way out to the Rembrandt Hotel in Hollywood, where they were currently staying. Lucinda Rockwell's biological Father was a successful and prominent Atlanta businessman with money to burn. He had also worked as a Crypto-Linguist while serving in the Army's Counter-Intelligence Corps and it was through these old ties that he was referred to my company, Optimum Strategies Inc, for a more permanent form of justice for his daughter's attackers.

Now, here I was, on my way to the top entertainment outlet in the City of Angels to quickly complete the somewhat "rushed," last minute job that Optimum Strategies had assigned to me. I say that it was rushed because for the last few months all the best triggermen in our Firm had been working on a really huge, multi-million dollar contract in Houston and I'd agreed to take this job as a small detour before returning to H-Town in the Great State of Texas since no one else really could. Leaning back on the hard plastic seat, I feel the hilt of the short and sharp, but still airplane legal mini-stilleto knife tucked into the rear of my jeans.

I look at my watch as the Red Line slows and stops, the voice following the pleasant chimes announcing the arrival at Hollywood and Highland. It's 10:48 pm. I still had a forty minute window to make contact with my female weapons courier at the Arabian Nights strip club at 7180 West Sunset Boulevard. I step off the subway and hop onto the escalator, riding it up to where North Highland Avenue intersects Hollywood Boulevard. I hang a right at the top and walk into a bizarre world unto itself.

Hollywood is Skid Row meets Vaudeville. Hollywood Boulevard is a temporally isolated, electrically polished patchwork quilt of tourism landmarks, hole in the wall movie gimmick money traps and a squared off network of exponentially intimate apparel sex shops. These are flanked by dark alleys where a shadow can mean trouble. Hidden away in the dark of an overbearing urban nightscape, there's always somebody getting high, tweaked, blown, stoned or stabbed.

Hollywood is a chunk of concrete absinthe split open by parallel asphalt canyons. Each one is dotted with movie buff booby traps, reproduction enhancement centers, massage parlors and mid-level offices for movie companies. To this day, Hollywood is like a pleasure beacon for youngsters seeking fame. It beckons to them like a sexy woman clad in expensive jewelry and a velvet dress.

The truth is not so inviting.

In Hollywood, pretty, petite, female cornshuckers and Southeast Texas Prom Queens come to be starlets, but end up spreading their legs and sucking limp dicks to feed their crack habits. Hollywood is not the hot gal in the velvet dress, but a parasitic, makeup covered whore, wrapped in metal wrinkles and open, syphilitic sores. The Boulevard is a shattered dream avenue inside an entertainment Mecca.

Hollywood and Sunset Boulevards is the façade covered, Los Angeles fault line where the posh and the phony clash with the nasty and the genuine.

Looking up in the sky makes me feel like I'm on an urban colony inside a Black Hole surrounded by light studded mountains. At night, walking down Hollywood Boulevard feels a lot like trudging through a carnival freak show and wading through a legion of seemingly normal, alcohol powered zombies. East of the Kodak Theater, the streetside platoons of hole in the wall tourist traps seem to be infused with small clusters of kinky, sexual entertainment shops blaring music from the late eighties. Just down the street from a large

Disney store built to cater to children, a few scattered lingerie shops continue retailing intimate apparel that would make a New Orleans Pimp blush purple.

On any night in Hollywood Boulevard, you might pass a one of a kind T-Shirt store opposite a sex toy outlet with a model of an artificial pocket pussy behind a window, all just a few feet down from a silver plated statue of some golden age movie star.

Across the street near Graumann's Chinese Theater, four LAPD Patrolmen are arresting an Imperial Stormtrooper for kicking the crap out of Spiderman.

I cross over to North La Brea Avenue and follow it down to Sunset Boulevard where I take a right catty corner from a Burger King past an El Pollo Loco and stroll down to the Arabian Nights strip club to make contact with a green eyed stripper named Jade. According to the briefing that my boss, Mike Schramme, had given me, she would be making her lap dance rounds in a pair of red, Harem style see-through pants (these are the kind Harem girls are supposed to have worn way back when, the kind that let you see through the to the broad's underwear). I walk up to the entrance and pay twenty dollars to get in.

The technotronic, eardrum thumping dance music is blaring as you walk inside, shrouded in darkness until you get near the stage and glimpse the barely legal lust queen gyrating on the stage and stripping off her bra. Of course, none of the club's patrons pay you any attention. *Their* minds are focused on more desirable objects and fantasies.

Per the arrangement, you go to the bar and order a Corona for eight fucking dollars and scratch your head a couple of times. A minute later, a made in heaven fuck bunny strides up next to you and sits down. She has piercing green eyes that look like freckled jades and a svelte body that makes you want to say, "fuck this hitman shit" and take a rough, wet ride in her lower guts. She asks you to buy her a drink and you agree. She smells like a scented bra at a French Lingerie Store.

You follow her to the inside of a booth in the back. She draws the booth's curtain shut and says, "just wait right here sweetie." You do just that since you're horny and you've got a job to do.

Holy shit, I want to screw this gal so fucking bad. Oh fucking well.

When she returns, she quietly asks, "Were you followed?"

I say, "no, I ran counter-surveillance routes and I'm clean. You got what I need?"

"Yeah," she says before dropping a nylon duffel bag at my feet.

"It's all there."

I unzip the bag and start to pull out my gear. It's all there, the pistol, the silencer, the new set of clothes, the ammo, everything.

I strip off my jacket, jeans and gray T-Shirt and slip into a cheap, three-piece suit with no ties and a pair of black tennis shoes. I stick on a phony goatee and use water and a comb to slick back my hair. Jade hands me a cup of the same hair coloring fluid she and others in her profession occasionally use to color their streamlined pussy hairs. She helps me comb it in and after a few minutes, my coarse, jet black hair has been turned into a very light brown, the same as my fake goatee. Then, I put on the small but still a little "geeky" looking eyeglasses. I slip the shoulder holster on underneath the sport coat and check to make sure that the holder for the silencer is taped in place behind it. I slip on the black gloves at the bottom of the duffel bag and remove my last three additional tools; an aptly named "Self Defense Pencil," a short, compact, .40 caliber Walther P99 pistol sporting a laser sight, all of it in dark black finish with serial numbers wiped away with hydrochloric acid. Alongside it are two magazines of subsonic, hollow point ammunition, a Sionics Silencer and a Surefire Kroma flashlight. This model of Surefire flashlight, like many others, was small enough to fit in the palm of a man's hand yet, at a rating of 50 Lumens for its intensity, was more than powerful enough to temporarily blind a man at close range, even in daytime. It and others like it, was a perfect addition for any professional shooter or police officer's self-defense arsenal. With a push button switch at the back, it was a quick, fast, multi-tasked, effective tool. Beneath it is a small, black, Trac-Phone, i.e. an untraceable cell phone.

The "Self Defense Pencil" wasn't really a pencil at all. It looked just like any other stylish, expensive, Cross Pen but instead of a ballpoint pen tube, it contained a thick, sturdy, carbide steel tube shaped like a heavy gauge hypodermic needle with a razor sharp tip at the end. When the top of the pen was clicked over in a clockwise direction, the sharpened steel rod would shoot out with enough pressure to easily puncture flesh and tissue. Then, it could still be used as a lengthy stabbing implement.

As for the pistol magazines, while their max capacity is 10 rounds, I've loaded them with eight since so many jams are due to magazine stoppages. This will give their springs more pushing power and help prevent this from occurring.

After screwing on the Sionics silencer, I carefully insert an eight round magazine into the pistol grip of the Walther before pulling back the slide and chambering a round. I holster it and accept the tiny communications piece that Jade hands me. I slip it in my right ear and ask her: "So, what's the latest on the two Marks?"

She responds professionally with the info my associates, Tom Heckler and Chas Beveridge, would've been passing her while they kept an eye on the Rembrandt Hotel.

"Same as a few hours ago. They're still in Room 212, sleeping like babies after fucking like cracked out rabbits. They ordered up for room service about an hour ago. So far, no one's been sneaking around the inside of the hotel and the extradition warrant from Atlanta still hasn't come through. Still, there's two plainclothes LAPD cops-might be Detectives but not for sure-that have parked outside the hotel's main entrance and have been keeping an eye on comings and goings in the main Lobby. And, there's a patrol car parked outside of the rear exit."

I ask her what the two plainclothes cops look like.

"One's tall and blonde, sort of muscular with a mild crewcut wearing a sweatshirt and jeans and the other guy is in a three piece suit with a black tie. He's got brown hair and he's about medium height."

I say, "What about the room?"

She says, "The curtains were drawn shut and the lights are still off."

While pulling out and pocketing the Hotel master card-key that Heckler had "covertly obtained," I say, "Do you have the briefcase and the carry on luggage?"

Jade just reaches underneath the booth's chair and pulls out a brown leather Samsonite briefcase with a laptop inside and a heavy duty carry on bag filled with spare clothes and toiletries. If by some chance I had any trouble with those cops posted outside, I'd use the briefcase contents and the carry on along with my plane ticket from Dallas Ft. Worth's Love Field to work my traveling businessman cover angle. There was already a room in my fake name of Jack Stoup with the cover credentials to go with it. As for getting into Billy Ray Cobb's room, the master key would come in handy, but I'll stay prepared to try another way first since it was almost a guarantee that the Hotel tracked their use and may have changed or updated the system after this one was stolen. We'll just have to see. While I make ready with the tiny amount of corporate baggage, Jade passes me an LAPD badge with phony credentials. I pocket these knowing they might become necessary if some cop stopped me while I was still carrying the Walther. The silencer would be tough to explain, but fuck it, I'd think of something if I have to and besides, Tom and Chas would be nearby to back me up if need be. I look back at Jade.

I say, "Anything else?"

She grimaces and says, "Not right now, but I'll be waiting for you when you're done. You ready?"

I nod my head and after stuffing my old set of clothes in the black duffel bag she disappears for a few seconds to secure it with her personal items and reappears. I follow her to a secluded rear exit that only she and other employees have easy access to. She lets me out and says, "come back soon." I walk outside and stroll towards the Saharan Desert Inn and hail a Taxi. I tell the driver, who sounds Armenian, that my name is Mike Sanchez and to quickly take me up to the Rembrandt Hotel at 1755 North Highland Avenue. He accepts and we're off.

We go back up North La Brea and take a more scenic route east on Hollywood Boulevard before going north on North Las Palmas Avenue and left on Yucca Street. This longer, less direct route, with a few abrupt stops, twists and turns, gives me a chance to see if I'm being tailed. So far, so good.

When we arrive I pay the twenty-three dollar fee and toss in a five for a tip.

The driver says, "Ok, tanks my main man buddy" and drives off.

I stroll into the Rembrandt Hotel's main entrance after steeling a quick glance around the outside to see if I can spot the two LAPD cops eyeing the location of my targets. I was just about to give it up for fear of looking suspicious when I spotted it. A plain Crown Victoria, similar to those used by numerous police department's, parked catty corner from the entrance where it could remain fairly well secluded and still have a clear, wide field of view around the Hotel's side and front. The empty, crumpled coffee cups and discarded candy wrappers piled on the dashboard make it obvious that the vehicle's occupants have been sitting inside it for a very long time. Of course, if it belonged to a Hotel employee or a transient, white-collar corporate type it most likely would not have had such food containing garbage placed on the dashboard. The guy on the passenger seat reading a newspaper looks a lot like one of the descriptions Jade gave me. That means the other one is inside somewhere waiting in the lobby or stalking around outside. To blend in with another platoon of corporate yuppies coming my way, I pretend that I hear my cell phone ringing and pull it out of an inner pocket on the right of my sport coat. Pretending to be holding an important conversation, I yammer away on it and trot inside, occasionally faking cellular interference so I can appear convincingly puzzled in order to grab quick glances around to try and spot the other cop.

Shit, I can't find him.

Then, as I push into the elevator with everyone else and click off my cell, I spot a somewhat short, heavyset man on the other side of the lobby also reading a paper. He's using his peripheral vision to watch another elevator disgorging more patrons. Before the door closes, I notice that one of the older men working behind the check in desk is doing the same thing. He has well groomed, close cropped gray hair and is obviously toned up and in good shape. He's got that veteran or ex-cop/military presence about him. Shit, LAPD must've stuck one of their own among the Hotel staff. Well, fuck it, that was nothing unusual. LAPD were definitely *not* amateurs.

The doors close and I hit a button for the second floor.

When the doors open with a pleasant chime I hang a right and walk down to room 212 and I'm about to withdraw the card key when I see a bell hop walking my way. According to what Tom and Chas found out, these guys carried master keys but had to log it in after each use just in case. Yeah, just in case a guy like me showed up. Suddenly, my earpiece buzzes and I hear Tom saying, "all's quiet on the Western Front." That meant nothing had changed and they were still asleep. Good to go.

I stick my hand in the air and plead with him to open the door to 212.

"Excuse me sir, I ah, feel sorta dumb askin' you this, but could you open my door for me? It's room 212. I feel really stupid, but I kinda forgot my card key when I left to go to a meeting this afternoon. I don't think my girlfriend Bobby is in there, 'cause I called earlier and she didn't answer, musta went out for Chinese or something. My name's Billy Cobb and like I said, I don't wanna sound like an idiot, but, could you open it for me?"

"Uhm, oh yeah, sure, but I'll have to call my boss and see if that room is in your name. It'll just take a second."

He asks if a Billy Cobb had rented this room and his boss must've said yes because he just smiled back and said, "sure thing sir."

I gotta move fast.

As he swipes the card key and opens the door I feel my palms sweat a little inside the black gloves. It's pitch dark inside. I look down the hall to make sure it's clear and I leap at the bellboy, ramming my right knee into his groin and slamming my right hand into his nose and clamping down on his mouth. I dig my two longest fingers into his eye sockets as his face turns dark crimson from the pain and shock. His knees go week and I slam his head back and down towards the floor while sweeping his right leg out from under him. As he falls and hits the floor, I shut the door and toss my luggage on the carpet. A rustling sound to my left indicates that my two targets are starting to wake.

There is still enough ambient light seeping through the curtains to make out where the bellboy's head is. I pull out the silenced Walther and click on the bright green laser sight, edging it up to where his head catches a tiny ray of sodium vapor light and pull the trigger twice.

POP *CRAACK*, SPLAT, POP *CRAACK*, SPLAT.

The hollow points bore through his skull and toss bone and brain matter onto the carpet underneath him. This fucker is dead.

I hear what must be Bobby Joe Wilson's voice squeeking; "Billy, Billy Ray, turn on da' lats, there somethin' ain'r rat, someone's here!"

I drop down to one knee and aim the pistol down, listening to exactly where her voice is. I hear Billy Ray Cobb.

"Goddamit, who's there, sumbitch, who da' fuck's there?"

I hear him fumbling for the lamp. Oh fucking shit, this would might cast a shadow that could be seen from outside. Now it was too late.

Billy switches the nightstand lamp on and since as the girl, Bobby Joe is more likely to scream, I kill her first by aiming the laser sight in between her bare, banana looking tits and squeeze off two shots center mass. Small gouts of blood explode from her chest and she slumps down, starting to twitch.

Billy Ray tenses and says, "OH MOTHERFUCKIN SHIT!"

He frantically reaches into the nightstand and I pull the trigger three times, sending a string of .40 caliber round into his face and head. His jawbone shatters as a tiny cauldron of bone, blood and brain matter appear on the wall behind the bed. I crawl around to the other side and put one round into Bobby Joe Wilson's forehead, just to make sure the bitch is as dead as a French drag queen at a southeast Mississippi Klan rally. Son of a bitch, I'd hate to get a blowjob from this young hag.

Her teeth were so bucked out and fucked up it looked like she could eat watermelon through a picket fence.

I crawl around on the floor, police up my briefcase and carry on and look down at the deceased bell hop.

POP CRAACK, POP CRAACK.

Two more rounds drill through his head. It pays to be thorough in my line of work. I slip out the empty magazine, pocket it and insert another, jacking a round in the chamber before re-holstering the Walther. It was time to beat feat away from ground zero. I hear no one in the hall, so I open up the door, turn into the hallway and exit out of another elevator.

Once outside, I casually walk down Yucca Street to get picked up by Tom Heckler and Chas Beveridge. Everything's going just fine until I see a blur out of my peripheral vision. I smell a nostril assaulting odor wave of shit, marijuana and alcohol right before a gleam of metal flashes in front of my eyes as a switchblade is snapped open. I should've been paying more attention to what was in front of me instead of worrying about two cops that might come running from behind me.

Standing before me is the urban dictionary definition of a hopeless, junkie/ tweeker. While waving the knife around, he yells, "GIVE ME YOUR FUCKIN' MONEY MAN OR I SWEAR TO FUCKIN' GOD I'LL CUT YOU, I'LL CUT YOU MAN, GIVE ME YOUR GODDAMN WALLET AND YOUR SHIT OR I'LL GUT YOU, YOU YUPPIE ASSHOLE…!

He looks like someone whose Neanderthal mother was raped by a mythical sewage monster. Touching this pathetic asshole could land you in a hospital isolation ward for infectious diseases. Fuck this humanoid punk, he needed to be put out of his misery.

Pretending to be scared, I say, "hey, hey man, alright, I'll give ya' my wallet and my laptop, ok, just please don't kill me man, alright?"

I toss my briefcase and carry on bag at him and say, "alright here's my wallet, just please don't kill me." I move like I'm going for my wallet but grab the Surefire Kroma with my left hand while edging my right to my other pocket where I'd put my"Self-Defense Pistol." Quickly moving away from him before jerking my left hand up in the air, I push the rear button on the Surefire, blasting the ultra-intense light right into his pupils which were already dilated from both the night and "reefer toking." He spasms and screams like a wild animal, twisting around to the right to look away from me and that's when I move in to fuck him up. In the initial shock, he's lost his tight grip on the knife and I leap forward, burying the empty end of the pencil into his left eye socket and slamming the Surefire into the side his skull, a resounding *crack* resulting from the impact. I use my thumb to twist the stabbing pencil's top halfway around and with a wet snapping sound, the carbide steel tube shoots out deep into the punk's brain. I let the Surefire hang loose on its little lanyard as I grip the base of his skull with my left hand and push the steel needle further in while ramming my right knee into his scrotum. I drive up at an angle to get it deeper into the worthless prick's brain, or whatever the fuck was left of it.

I jerk the pencil out, put it in my left hand and pull out the pistol with my right. I place the silencer on top of his drooping, gore oozing head and pull the trigger once. The splatter spews some blood and brain on my shoes to complement what was already on my gloves. I holster the pistol, pick up my stuff and move on until I get near the intersection with North McCadden. Tom and Chas are waiting there in a red Pontiac. I hop in the back and I listen to the police band scanner hooked to the center console as they drive me back to Arabian Nights. Tom tosses me some Baby Wipes so I can start wiping off that "tweeker's" blood.

As we cruise down Sunset, the first calls come in for a dead bum on Yucca Street. Fuck him, who would care. On the way, we weave in and out of various dark alleys to dispose of my briefcase and carry on bag in separate dumpsters. We chuck the pistol, gloves, Surefire (what a waste of a good flashlight), stiletto and ammo down a back alley sewer on Schrader Boulevard. Tom talks into his cell phone once Chas brings up to a red light next to the Burger King on North La Brea. The light goes green and after we move through the intersection, Tom looks back and says, "she's waiting, so go back to that rear exit and she'll let you back in." I just nod and leap out when we get there.

They speed off to go bed down somewhere before grabbing their own next day flights back to Dallas Ft. Worth where we'd meet up again for our next really big and hopefully final, contract hit operation in Houston, which should allow damn near all of us in Optimum Strategies Inc, to finally retire.

I knock three times on the rear exit and Jade lets me in. We go back to the booth where we met before and I strip down to my boxers as she brings me my original set of clothes. I put them all back on and as I'm about to leave, she says, "hey, my shift's almost up, you need a ride to the airport?"

Well, it was so late the Subway might not even be operating, so what the hell, my boss Mike Schramme had checked this broad out and said she was good to go. For now, that is. So, I answer in the affirmative and in about fifteen minutes we're cruising south on the 405 freeway towards LAX in her white Ford Mustang. It felt good to be gettibg away from any areas near the "hit" even though it had been well thought out for such short notice. All that the club manager or bouncer would know is that I came in, stayed a long time in the back with Jade and then left in the same outfit I was in when I arrived.

I suppose I could talk nice to her but in the end, what would be the point.

I tell her to drop me off at the Four Points Sheraton on Airport Boulevard and after I step out of the car, I find myself smirking as she drives off. It's a shame she didn't get a chance to really enjoy the money we paid her for being a courier. Like most of the hot, snotty bitches that populated this socialist state, she obviously loved money and besides, she'd seen too damn much as far as we were concerned. That's why my old Rhodesian Merc buddy Mike Hester was waiting inside her apartment on Melrose Avenue to "cancel her contract." I breathe a sigh of relief when I walk into the Sheraton, knowing that a nice, plush warm bed set up by the hotel's room service professionals was waiting for me.

Two mornings later, I wake at 5:30 am for my 6:45 am flight back to Dallas Ft. Worth. While going through security, I notice that LAPD Patrolmen have replaced the T.S.A. Supervisors that usually sit behind podiums to watch the "screening process." Based on what I'd heard, this had happened around August twenty-fifth of this year. Supposedly, it had something to do with LAPD getting a hold of documents from T.S.A. files recording the screeners sexually assaulting female passengers in late 2004 and early 2005. No surprise there. They always seemed preoccupied with feeling up or patting down hot, young girls and old ladies (as if that would protect anyone from a bunch of Middle Eastern Islamic psychos). Hell, all the idiotic passenger searching and groping won't do a goddamn thing to stop a pack of rag head lunatics from firing off Surface-to-Air missiles at any number of planes during takeoff and landing. What a fucking joke. Their procedures make hardened professional killers and infiltrators such as yours truly, laugh like crazy.

After arriving in Dallas, I hooked up with Chas, Tom, and Mike Hester before driving down to Houston, good old H-Town. Only the million we'd make off this last hit can keep some old bittersweet, yet painful memories from welling up inside me. Deep down, I just wanted to go down there, kill the next batch of assholes and get the fuck out. We'd planned for over a year and everything was in place except for us. A "piece of cake" I kept thinking. I guess we'll see...

THE END...for now.

ENDNOTES

[1] This MOS or Military Occupational Specialty is given the number designation 0351. Marines in this MOS are trained in both explosives employment as well as use of the 83mm SMAW Rocket for both anti-tank and various Urban or bunker destruction tasks.

[2] The U.S. began employing Thermobaric munitions in Afghanistan in 2001 as a way to more effectively kill Taliban terrorists hiding in caves. These types of munitions proved to be ideal for such scenarios because their effects are actually increased in enclosed spaces with limited oxygen.

[3] This type of tank armor is comprised of an explosive charge placed in between a pair of ceramic plates. Once struck, it detonates in order to counter the effect of a shaped charge warhead.

[4] Sodium Thiopental is a relatively concentrated chemical designed to rapidly induce unconsciousness

[5] Term From Wikipedia

[6] What I describe with regards to Angela and Tammy's experiences is in fact a mixture of three factual, separate incidents of abuse perpetrated by the T.S.A. at Denver and Reagan International Airports. At Denver, a 12 year old girl was stripped without the presence of her father and one woman's breasts were damaged after a screener yanked out some of the staples. At Reagan, ABC-7 of Washington D.C. reported on Illegal Strip Searches at D.C.A. where one woman was forced by screeners to "duck walk" naked.

CPSIA information can be obtained at www.ICGtesting.com
Printed in the USA
LVOW040510030812

292718LV00003B/73/P

9 781606 106426